Final Assignment

a novel by

Phillips Wylly

Novels by Phillips Wylly

STATEN ISLAND

The mob moves into the world of Entertainment

HOLLYWOOD'S BEST

A boy and a girl seeking fame and fortune
learn success comes with a price

Dedication

For Shirley Winter who sometimes allows people to call her Shirley Wylly. I call her my wife and my love.

April

Washington, DC

IF YOU CLICK on "Google Maps" you can learn the distance from downtown DC to Dulles International Airport is 28.6 miles and the travel time is 40 minutes, 60 minutes if there is traffic. G1 Specialist John Gunner didn't know where they measured that 28.6 miles from and he had no idea what time of day or night they made the trip in 40 minutes, "60 minutes if there's traffic," all he knew was he left the office at 2PM and thanks to a sudden "April Shower" down pour that had completely fucked up traffic he was not at all sure he could make Dulles in time to setup and be ready for Sheik al-Sameur's 5:20 arrival.

"You damn well better be," he told himself. This was his fourth assignment, but his first stateside and there could be no excuse for failure.

A very average looking man, maybe even less than "average," John Gunner had no distinguishing features. He was a shade under six feet in height, he weighed 170 pounds, his hair was sort of brown, not blond, not black, just what some people call "dirty blond," and at this particular moment in his life he wore a kind of fuzzy beard which did nothing to make his non-descript face more, or less, attractive. Were you to meet him in a group of people he would be the one you would not remember - unless you looked into his eyes, really looked into them that is. There is something about his eyes that is memorable, even slightly frightening. They are average like everything else about him, dark - probably blue - but they seem devoid of all feeling, all expression. Even when he smiles, or seems to smile, his eyes don't, they just look empty. His eyes had not always this way. Once upon a time his eyes had been bright, eager, filled with the youthful excitement of life. That was long ago, before he understood the meaning of the word "tragedy."

After what seemed like forever he finally reached the George Washington Parkway and traffic began to move a bit faster, actually getting up to 35 miles an hour once or twice. He guessed he would be able to make the airport in time after all, and he began to relax a little.

As always, there was a long line of cars and busses trying to get into Dulles. Fortunately his van was taller than the two sedans in front of it and a cop up ahead spotted the "TVNews.Gov" logo painted above the wind screen. The officer held up traffic, waved him around the lineup and into the "Press" parking lot. He waved and mouthed "Thank you," to the cop as he passed him and couldn't help smiling as he thought to himself, what better cover could he possibly have than being a TV News cameraman?

Except for the traffic getting in and out of the place, Gunner always found working at Dulles a pleasure. They did a great job for the press. The interview rooms were usually on the second floor with soundproof sliding doors opening onto a balcony overlooking the airport from where they could photograph plane arrivals. Inside, the rooms were always setup with good lighting and a lectern fitted with a single microphone that had plug-ins for everybody's use to record whatever remarks the arriving VIP might make.

Two other news crews were loading equipment into an airport jitney as Gunner pulled into a spot next to the NBC TV van. His equipment was so light-weight he could easily handle it by himself and it took him only a minute to load everything he needed into the baggage bin and find a seat next to Tom Wilson, a cameraman for a cable news network, who frequently turned up at the same events as he did. They had become casual friends.

"Hi John, how's it going?" Wilson stuck out his fist for a welcoming bump.

"Fine by me, Tom, but how's that boy of your's?" The last time Gunner had seen Wilson he learned the youngster had the measles. The jitney reached the terminal building and they had taken the elevator up to the interview room before Tom finished telling him how well the boy was getting on.

Gunner set up his tri-pod and measured the distance to the lectern. Seventeen feet. Add two, perhaps two and a half feet more to where the Sheik would stand, at the most he was looking at twenty feet. No problem, anything under thirty feet, even thirty-five feet was safe. Twenty feet was a snap unless something got in the way, something like a layer of heavy cloth. If the Sheik was wrapped up in one of those burnoose things, with a loose hood covering half his face, that could be a problem.

Surprisingly, in spite of the earlier rain squalls the Sheik's plane was actually a few minutes early. Together with ABC, CNN, NBC, and CableNews, Gunner trooped out onto the balcony to photograph the arrival of the Afghanistan Air Bus as it pulled up to the gangway. Moments later, de-barking completed and recorded, the news crews trooped back inside to await the appearance of today's distinguished visitor. After less than five minutes the door next to the lectern opened and a State Department type, followed by several burnoose-wearing men, came into the room. The Arabs looked around suspiciously while the State Department man stepped up to the lectern.

"Ladies and Gentlemen, may I present Sheik Jamil al-Sameur."

Gunner switched on his camera as the Arabs made an aisle for the Sheik. "I wish to Christ I could take care of all you bastards," he told himself. But he couldn't… He put his eye in the finder and focused on the doorway as the Sheik entered.

"Hot damn!" He tried to suppress a smile as he spoke to himself. The sheik was wearing a business suit. No problem.

Jamil al-Sameur had very little to say: He was pleased to be in the beautiful city of Washington, DC. He was looking forward to meeting with Senator Anderson and the senate committee. He smiled, he nodded, he waved and posed for the cameras.

"Wait," John told himself as he centered the cross hairs on the sheik's nose and thought of his father and his brother and his mother. "Wait until he starts out of the room... Okay, now, and fuck you Sheik Sameur."

It usually took five to six seconds... "One... two... three...four," John counted to himself. The poor bastard didn't even know he was already dead. "Five…" The sheik was almost to the doorway when he stumbled slightly before disappearing ahead of the group following him.

"Help!... Help!... Doctor. Help!"

Everyone in the room scrambled to find out what was happening. The Sheik's people tried to block them but to no avail. Like everyone else Gunner lifted his camera high over his head and took pictures of the sheik crumpled on the hallway floor.

George Washington Parkway

IT WAS AFTER seven o'clock when John Gunner backed his van out of the parking spot and headed towards the exit. Another thunder storm had rolled in from somewhere and rain was again tying up traffic. All the cars that had been lined up waiting to get into the airport when he arrived now seemed to be lined up waiting to get out of the place too. "Go figure," he muttered, but thanks to the miracle of electronics he had no need to hurry. There was a time when Newsreel Cameramen had to rush their film back to the lab for processing, now it was all high speed electronic transmission. At the same time his camera made a recording it sent the image back to the newsroom. No more hustling helicopters, no more careening motorcycles, today when you shot a story it could be edited and on the air before you could pack up and get back to your car.

As soon as he reached the highway he telephoned the news room.

"Good job, John," His boss told him. "Would you like me to set up a Dubai Account for you this time, or do you still want cash?"

"I'd rather have the money one more time please, Harry. Come number five, and the bonus, maybe it will be time to start that account, but not yet."

"Okay," Harry chuckled, "Money plays. Where are you now?"

"Just got out of the airport," Gunner answered, "It's raining like hell and traffic is truly slammed!"

"Oh my. That will make it after eight o'clock before you can get back here and I'm due at the press club dinner before that. Why don't you just go on home tonight, we'll get together in the morning."

Resisting the instinct to answer "Yes Sir," Gunner told him, "Sounds good to me," he could wait until morning to receive his $10,000 fee. It had been nearly four years since he attended West Point but the training still manifested itself in many ways and the need to address officers as "Sir" was one of them and "Harry" was, in fact, Colonel Harold Gustafson, Specialist John Gunner's commanding officer. He knew the colonel thought he was foolish to keep so much cash on hand but there was something about having actual cash that made him feel good. With the fee he would collect in the morning he would have better than $55,000 in his safe. He was not all that comfortable with the idea of having his money in an account in some far off country.

He had almost reached the Arlington National Cemetery before the rain slacked off and traffic began to move more freely. The National Cemetery was established in Arlington, Virginia, during the Civil War, on the grounds of what was the estate of Robert E. Lee's wife's family. Since then more than 300,000 Veterans and military casualties from every one of the nations' wars, many together with their spouses, have been buried there. Just seeing the name "Arlington Cemetery" on the roadside sign in his headlights brought sad memories to John Gunner's mind because included in those 300,000 casualties were his father, his mother and his brother. Victims of Arab terrorism. They were the reason he had joined Group One. They were the reason he had welcomed this afternoon's assignment.

1147 Cherry Avenue

AFTER FINDING A SPOT to park the van right in front of the two story center hall "garden apartment" building he called home, John Gunner carefully lifted his camera equipment out of the back of the van. He never ever left equipment in the van, car theft was not a common problem here on Cherry Avenue, but with specialized equipment like his you never, never took chances. Gathering his equipment under one arm, he pressed the remote "lock" button, heard the acknowledging "beep," then headed for the building.

His second floor apartment boasted an excellent kitchen, a comfortable bedroom and bath, and a spacious living room, complete with a fireplace and a tiny balcony, that overlooked the two miniature cherry trees standing in the front yard. "Hello fish," he called as he stepped through his front door. Gunner often wondered how many men his age counted tropical fish as their best friends. Not too many he guessed, but in his line of work you weren't likely to have too many friends. Best if you didn't. I'm a secret, I don't exist, he often reminded himself. You start getting to know people, they start getting to know you, and before you know it they find out things they shouldn't; then suddenly your friend has become a "security risk," and we can't have security risks.

Dogs and cats could be safe friends, but you couldn't leave them alone for very long and at any moment he was likely to be sent to God knew where: Europe, the middle east, South America, wherever. That was the news business; that was G1 business. So the fish. The automatic feeder could take care of the fish for up to ten days, beyond that his landlord, Mr. Ludenthal, was happy to add water to the tank and put fresh food in the dispenser until he returned. As for the fish, well they were in a world of their own. They didn't give a damn about who fed them, but they were something to have around, something to make the place a home, and every now and then he did think the large angel fish looked back through the glass at him with something of a sign of recognition.

Okay, fish are safe, he told himself, so what about Beryl?

Beryl… Beryl Kinney, the new tenant across the hall in Apartment #3. What strange bit of luck brought her into his life? Or was it luck? The colonel had made a point of warning him about strangers. Not once or twice, but almost constantly. "Remember you're a secret. What you do is highly confidential. Strangers who want to be friends are suspect." And Beryl Kinney was certainly a stranger who seemed to want to be a friend. Less than an month ago he had been minding his own business one evening, trying to unlock his front door with a bag of groceries in one hand and his keys in the other, when a voice, a woman's voice, came from behind him.

"Mr. Ludenthaul says you collect tropical fish."

Surprised, he turned slightly to look back over his shoulder and there she was, standing in the door to the apartment across the hall. Medium height, dark hair, nice figure, not beautiful maybe but "interesting" looking. He had been aware a new renter had moved in across the hall from him but until that moment he had not seen her.

"I do too," she continued. "I'll show you mine if you show me yours."

He almost dropped the bag of groceries.

"Oh-oh, look out." Seeing his plight she hurried to his side just in time to catch the bunch of bananas that were half way out of his grocery bag. Then, standing quite close to him, with one hand still holding the bananas, she smiled and said, "Hi. I'm Beryl Kinney, your new neighbor." Since then, she had invited him to dinner and to see her fish, he had reciprocated by inviting her to have a drink and see his. That led to taking her to dinner down the street at the DC Grill, and three days after that to a ball game up in Philadelphia. He had learned she was a Computer Technician at the Federal Aviation Administration and he had told her something about his life as a TV News Cameraman. And this growing friendship, John Gunner knew very well, was not something to be encouraged. No, it was something that should be reorted to the colonel, something Harry would not be happy to learn about because friends, particularly girlfriends, could become security risks. It was a relationship that should be reported to the colonel and discontinued immediately.

That's absolutely correct! He agreed with himself as he stored the camera gear in the hall closet then returned to the fish tank. "Okay fish, time for dinner." He glanced at his wristwatch as he gave them a pinch of food. After nine o'clock, he should probably get something to eat too.

The knock on his front door and her voice calling "John," interrupted his thoughts. "Were you there?"

"Was I where?" He asked as he opened the door..

"At the airport; where that man died," she answered. Then, "Can I come in?"

"Sure." He held the door open for her as he asked, "You mean the Sheik? Yeah, I was there."

She waited until he closed the door then, obviously upset, moved close to him and rested her head on his chest. He could feel her trembling and he put his arms around her. "You just never know, do you?" She whispered.

"Never know what?"

"You never know when it will be all over," she answered. "That man, al-Sameur, he wasn't very old. He just got off an airplane, a million miles away from home, and suddenly died. I saw it on the news. It must have been awful being there."

A dozen thoughts flashed through Gunner's mind but none of them seemed appropriate, so he just held her tight and waited for her to stop trembling.

"I don't want to be alone tonight," she said after a moment. Her voice, almost a whisper, was muffled by his chest. "Can I stay with you?"

He kissed the top of her head and told her everything would be okay and she was welcome to stay as long as she liked..

After a moment she leaned back and looked up at him. "You just got home didn't you?. It's almost ten o'clock and I bet you haven't had a thing to eat."

He started to answer but only had time to shake his head before she added, "I've got something in the fridge. You go take a hot shower and relax while I warm it up. I'll be right back."

"Beryl, you don't need..." No use, she was already out the door.

He was awake. She was sleeping soundly right there next to him, but he was awake. He pressed the button on his wrist watch to light up the dial: 3:45. He wasn't sure what had awakened him, just worry probably. Being with her had been good, but it wasn't something he should have done. The colonel had cautioned him time and time again about unexpected new friends, especially women friends. The colonel had given him the phone number of an agency that could provide great looking women... women who didn't have any interest in what he did or how he did it. Women who were safe. So what was Beryl Kinney doing here in his bed? Why did she want to know if he had been there, if he had covered al-Sameur's arrival. Why did she want to know that? Aw shit, he thought, this is ridiculous! She knows I'm a TV Cameraman, I cover news events, she figured I might have been there. That's logical. The guy dropping dead shook her up. She needed a little reassurance, a little comforting. What's so unusual about that? Nothing, he decided. Still, he should probably tell the colonel…

It was seven AM next time he looked at his watch. Thanks to the shades and drapes the room was still dark and Beryl was still sound asleep. Being as quiet as possible, Gunner slid out of bed, grabbed up some clothing and made his way to the bathroom without waking her. Twenty minutes later when he emerged, showered, shaved, and dressed for work, he found her sitting up in bed.

"Sorry, I didn't mean to wake you up," he told her. "I got-a go to work. You go back to sleep."

She yawned, stretched and swung her legs out of bed. "I have to go to work too."

"What-ever," he told her. "Bathroom's all yours. I got-at run."

As John Gunner left his apartment Beryl Kinney got out of bed and went to the living room window overlooking Cherry Avenue. She watched as he loaded his camera gear into the TVNews Van, got in and drove away. She did not think John Gunner was the type man who would leave behind something he needed but she waited several moments just to be sure; then, convinced he would not be returning, she went from room to room carefully looking into drawers and closets. The bedroom closet revealed an object of interest, a small safe. She quickly entered the make, model and serial number on her i-Phix, seconds later she received the entry code.

Apartment C - 1147 Cherry Avenue

"*HELLO AUNT SARAH,*" Beryl typed very carefully. It had taken her more than half an hour to prepare the coded message within the note to her "Aunt Sarah." It was sometimes difficult to work confidential information into chit-chat about things like seeing the first robin, new buds on the cherry trees and shopping for shoes:

Subject safe contains $45G cash,
Revolver, ammunition.
Driver License, Soc Sec card,
Passport for Albert Helms,
1175 Valencia Ave. SI. NY 10310

She re-read the message, doubled checked it against the handwritten original it had taken her so long to create, then clicked "SEND." Eleven minutes later "Aunt Sarah" responded. Within "her" words expressing delight at Beryl's new shoes was the message:

Excellent work.
Helms Passport & ID Fake
address does not exist.
Continue Investigation.

May

Apartment D - 1147 Cherry Avenue

LAST NIGHT it had been well after 1 AM when John Gunner finally got to bed. May was always a very busy month for TVNews.Gov. Its very existence, its reason for being, was to cover the activities of members of congress and government officials and May was the time when every representative and every senator was anxious to deliver video commencement speeches to the too many to visit schools and colleges back home. Added to that, the demands of Armed Forces Day, and later in the month Memorial Day made May "hell month." In the past two weeks John Gunner had not had time for even a quick drink with Beryl.

This night it seemed as if he had just gotten to sleep when the alarm sounded. He reached out for the clock and tried to turn it off then realized it wasn't the clock, it was his telephone.
"...Hello...yes?" He looked at the clock: almost six.

"John, this is Harry." The voice on the phone sounded too intense for this time of the morning.

He began to wake up. "Yes sir. Good morning."

"John, I'm sorry to call you this early but something has come up and I need you here ASAP."

"Yeah, okay. It's all right Harry. I'll be there as soon as I can shower and get dressed."

"Never mind the shower, John. Nobody is going to worry about how you smell. I need you here."

"Okay. On my way."

Gunner did not consider the five minute cold shower a case of disobedience so much as a requirement to wake himself up. He more than made up the time by dressing very quickly and driving very fast.

Office -TVNews.Gov

"SIT DOWN, JOHN." The colonel gestured towards the chair in front of his desk. In many ways Harry Gustafson thought of John Gunner as the son he would never have. A son like John would be wonderful. A son who, much like himself, loved his country and would willingly give his life to defend it. The order he must deliver to him was not easy to give.

"I have an assignment for you." The way the colonel said "assignment" told Gunner what kind of assignment it would be. "This will be number five and that means a twenty-five thousand dollar bonus, John." The colonel managed a brief smile before continuing. "But this one is going to be tough." The smile disappeared as he added, "You need to be in Senator Anderson's office by seven thirty."

"Senator Anderson's office?" Gunner's voice echoed his surprise. "What's the target?"

The colonel's voice took on a hard edge as he answered, "Senator Anderson, John."

Gunner blinked, "Senator Anderson? The senator is my assignment?"

"Yes, John. Senator Orin Anderson."

"But he's an American, a United States Senator."

"Not all of our country's enemies are Islamists," Harry told him in a quiet, almost eerie voice as he reached into his desk drawer and carefully lifted out one of the tiny "EB" power packs. Except on careful examination the power pack looked exactly like the digital cards used to record on. "He's called a press briefing at eight AM." The colonel held the digital power pack out for Gunner to take. "You need to be on your way. Good luck with your mission."

Almost too stunned to speak, John muttered, "Yes sir," as he took the small card, carefully put it in his jacket pocket, stood, turned, and somewhat stiff legged, left the colonel's office.

Harry Gustafson waited until his office door closed behind the young man before taking a deep breath. Slowly, he exhaled in a sigh, placed his right elbow on the desk top, and lowered his head until his temple rested on his thumbs. Only twice before had an order come down to eliminate an American citizen: Almost five years ago a CIA Agent who was actually Arab by birth; then two years ago an Assistant Secretary in the Treasury Department. The Assistant Secretary had been born into an old, old American family. Until today, that had been the most difficult assignment. Now a United States Senator, Senator Orin Anderson. A man Harry knew casually and had admired for many years. A man who only a few years ago had been a candidate for his party's vice presidential nomination. How can this be? He wondered.

Difficult as it had been for him to give the order he knew for John Gunner carrying it out would be even more so.

Senate Office Building

"HEY JOHN, good to see you." Chip Young welcomed Gunner as he walked into Senator Anderson's conference room. A pleasant looking middle age man, a few pounds overweight and almost always wearing a slightly rumpled suit, Chip Young had been Senator Anderson's Administrative Assistant and Press Secretary since before Gunner joined Group 1. Young knew, and was known by, almost every reporter and news cameraman in DC.

Gunner shook Young's hand, mumbled something like "Good morning," to him, then began to set up his tripod and camera. He had no idea how he got here. His mind was completely numb. He was under orders to eliminate a United States Senator. A man who had been in the senate for more than thirty-five years. A man who had once been considered to be his party's candidate for vice president. A man who was admired and respected by everyone. How could he eliminate such a man? But he could not disobey an order. He had taken an oath. He had pledged his life.

Young brought him a cup of coffee. "John, you look like you can use this."

"Chip, thanks." He took a sip. "Yeah, I guess my mind's all over the place this morning."

"No prob-lem-oh," Chip told him. "It's a pretty early call, but you know the old man, he's still a farmer at heart, up before the sun starts to shine. He's got a busy day lined up and he wants to get a statement on tape before he does anything else." Chip glanced around the otherwise empty room, "Thank God you're here, it doesn't look like anybody else is going to cover." He cocked his eyebrow then added, "I'm sure the old man will remember this next time the networks want something from him."

As if to prove him wrong the conference room door opened almost before Chip finished the sentence and Tom Wilson came trudging in followed by his crew.

"Hope we're not too late, Chip. Traffic's brutal this morning. We'll be covering for the pool."

"Glad you're here, Tom. How 'bout some coffee..."

It was Young's turn to ask Wilson about his son. As Tom told Chip the latest news, John Gunner turned his attention back to his camera. Less than five minutes later Senator Anderson entered the room.

"Good morning everyone." The senator nodded, smiled and waved as he made his way to the microphone. "Tom, John, everybody, thank you for coming."

John Gunner stepped behind his camera, switched it on and focused on the senator. He placed the cross-hairs on Anderson's forehead. But the silver haired man in his view finder was not an Arab terrorist, he was a United States Senator from Minnesota. How could this assignment be right?…

"You can turn off your camera now Johnnie…"

Gunner blinked. Tom Wilson's laughing voice had startled him. Something had happened. The senator was leaving the room. He had not carried out his orders. He had not eliminated the senator. Shaking his head from side to side, hardly aware of what he was doing, he dismounted the camera, picked up the tripod and headed for the exit door.

“Hey John,” Chip Young called. “What’s your hurry? How ‘bout some breakfast?”

“Can’t Chip. Got-a run.” He almost reached the parking lot before his phone began to vibrate. He started to reach for it, then stopped. He knew it was the colonel. What could he tell him? What could he say? He had failed to carry out a direct order. That was deliberate disobedience, and there was only one penalty for disobedience.

TVNews.Gov Office

AS HARRY GUSTAFSON switched off one phone another began to ring. It was his private phone. He picked up the instrument, punched in the security code and said, “Yes sir?”

“What happened?”

He knew the voice, always a bit agitated, always slightly condescending. “I don’t know, sir. I’m trying to make contact now.”

“I must assume there is a problem,” the voice paused for a beat, then continued, “And problems must be eliminated immediately.”

“Yes sir,” Harry cleared his throat before continuing, “I understand.”

The phone went dead.

Holding the now silent phone in his hand, Harold Gustafson slowly shook his head from side to side. This was not the Group 1 he signed on for. After several seconds he turned his attention back to the phone in his hand and again clicked John Gunner’s number...

Parking Lot - Senate Office Building

GUNNER'S PHONE began vibrating again as he was walking from the Senate Office Building, across the press parking lot, to where his van was parked. Be careful, think things out before you answer, he told himself, but his brain was not working as well as he wished. He had not completed his assignment and that was all he could think about. There was no excusable reason for not doing so, nothing to prevent him from completing the assignment, no electronic failure, no loss of target. No, the failure was his and his alone. He simply did not squeeze the trigger. And that was neglect of duty. Disobedience! What to do now? Answer the phone, he told himself.

He put the phone to his ear. "Yes sir."

"John," the colonel's voice was low. "What happened?"

"I don't know, sir. I just blanked out. He walked in, I put the cross hairs on him, then the next thing I knew he was leaving the room..."

"Ummm." The colonel's groan interrupted his thoughts.

"Sir...what should I do?"

There was a pause before Harry answered. "John, I don't quite know. I need to think about it. Right now there is an order out on you. Right now you need to disappear."

"Disappear?"

“Yes, John. Dump your gear in the van and go someplace where we can‘t find you. Contact me in tomorrow, but right now disappear!”

“Leave my camera?” His camera was the most secret thing of all, did the colonel want him to leave it in the van?

“Yes. Leave it.” The colonel’s voice left no question. “I’ll pick it up. You disappear! Now!!”

Disappear! How the hell do you “disappear? Gunner wondered as he switched off his phone. Langhorn/Davis made that impossible, or damn near impossible.

Hardly realizing what he was doing, he loaded the camera and tri-pod into the van then took off his TVNews jacket and slid his belt from his trousers. The belt buckle contained a GPS device that kept the office aware of his location. He tossed the jacket, belt and keys into the van and was about to slam the door - no, wait, the still camera! The video camera is easy to spot, it has the TVNews.Gov logo on its side and the colonel said to leave it, but the still camera accommodates the same digital power card, the day could come when I might have need for that still camera he thought… Okay, take it. Get the power card from the video camera, load it into the still camera, and take it.

Telling the van “goodbye,” Gunner walked determinedly to the exit gates. The guards might wonder what he was doing walking out but he was carrying the still camera; they would probably think he was going to get a shot of the building if they thought about it at all. He waved to them and they waved back, he was a regular visitor, they did not question him. As he crossed the street and headed for a city bus stop his brain began to function: If he was going to disappear there were things in his safe he would need. He could be there in less than fifteen minutes. It didn’t seem likely they could have it covered this soon...

Manhasset, NY

ON LONG ISLAND'S NORTH SHORE the town of Manhasset seems to have been there ever since time began. The center of the town, along Main Street, boasts a Long Island Rail Road Station and a movie theatre, both probably built in the 1930s. Locals often laughingly tell visitors they are the newest buildings in town. However, an area along Northern Boulevard, known as the "Miracle Mile," is also a part of Manhasset and there a string of comparatively new buildings, for upper end stores and businesses, have grown up over the past thirty or forty years. One of those "new" buildings houses the very exclusive, very expensive Cypress Gallery, owned and operated by tall, slender, quietly reserved Stephen Hunter, a man thought of by his colleagues and friends to be someone devoted to a life of art and his art gallery. When asked to describe Stephen Hunter people usually spoke of the large, horn rimmed glasses he wore, glasses that seem to dominated his facial features. The gallery satisfied his love for works of art and gave him a reason to travel the world whenever he wished, more correctly whenever Group 1 wished, and this morning G1 had an assignment for him in Washington, DC to where it wished him to travel very quickly.

It had been almost five years since President Wadsworth had asked him to resign his CIA post and join G1. His CIA cover as an Art Dealer worked perfectly for the new assignment. Since joining G1 he had completed six missions. Four overseas, and together with Paul Savage, two here in the United States.

G1 had been different before the change in command; then orders came from a voice he knew rather than from the filtered, electronic voice he listened to earlier this morning. But the voice made little difference to him. Terse, unexpected orders might be upsetting to some, but not to Stephen Hunter. How orders were transmitted was not important, what counted was receiving them. He lived for them; lived for the thrill of seeking out a "target "and carefully eliminating it. He never gave thought to who the target was - a woman, a man - not important. A target was not a person, a target was only "IT," be it someone he never heard of or, like today, a United States Senator.

"Mr. Hunter, your taxi is here."

Ethel's voice startled him as he stood gazing through his trademark heavy horn rim glasses at the two Larry Miller paintings he had just put on display. It amazed him how such a fine California artist could have been overlooked by the art world for so long. Thanks almost entirely to himself, Miller's paintings, which he bought several of a number of years ago for less than $20,000 each, were now selling for $300,000 and more, making him far less dependent on the fees he received for assignments such as today's. None the less, the fees were good, but it was the excitement that he lived for.

Slowly taking his eyes away from the Miller paintings Stephen Hunter looked at his wrist watch. Yes, it was ten-thirty, the taxi was right on time. "Thank you Ethel," he called back to her. "Be right there…"

The ride to JFK Airport usually took about half an hour and his flight to Washington wasn't 'till 12:14, but Stephen Hunter knew, sure as God made little green apples, if you counted on making it there in half an hour they would have the road torn up and a detour that would make you late. He always preferred to be early, and getting there early would give him time for a bite of lunch at the surprisingly good restaurant located in the passenger terminal.

Apartment D - 1147 Cherry Avenue

"HELLO FISH." If they thought about such things Gunner assumed they would be surprised to see him home in mid-morning. He sprinkled a pinch of dry food on top of the water, they would be surprised at this early feeding too.

Not time for fish, he told himself. He needed to move quickly. He needed to get money from the safe, he needed the forged pass port, driver's license and Social Security card that were in there too. The pass port, license and SS card were souvenirs from an illegal immigration story he had photographed more than a year ago right here in DC. They were supposed to be props, but they looked so perfect he had decided to keep them. Now they might be useful; very useful. The .38 revolver, should he take the gun? No, he decided, the still camera was weapon enough. If they caught him the gun probably wouldn't do him much good and traveling with a gun could create a lot of problems.

Okay, enough already. There was an old Washington Redskins jacket and cap in the back of the closet and a canvas gym bag. He put the money, the still camera and his Albert Helms ID papers in, then filled it with underwear: socks, two shirts, running shorts, shoes, a pair of jeans. He pulled on the Redskins jacket and cap, then wrote a short note to Mr. Ludenthall asking him to look after the fish; he would be away for a while, not sure just when he would get back, and was enclosing next month's rent incase his trip was extended. He thought about leaving a note for Beryl, but on second thought decided it might be better not to. It was time to leave. Time to get away before they come looking. And he knew they would come.

City Bus #107

TWO BLOCKS from his home John Gunner climbed into a bus, settled back in the seat, rested the heavy gym bag on his lap and tried to get his brain in gear. The colonel told him to disappear. Just how do you do that, he wondered. Not that he stood out in a crowd, he was just an ordinary looking guy, girls didn't lift their eyebrows when he walked past, men didn't admire his size or strength, sometimes it was good not to be the best looking man in the world he thought, but that wouldn't prevent Security Central from finding him. How can anybody disappear with the FBI's National Security System watching over us? All of us. A hell of a system, it had been created by PeTraCo Research. Having video-taped two stories about Security Central and its Computer Center, he was very familiar with it and had no doubt his picture had been check loaded by now.

"Check Load" was supposed to be very carefully monitored in order to prevent any unnecessary invasions of privacy. What a crock! Thanks to the Langhorn/Davis bill that created National Security Central no one had any privacy anymore. While all public outcry was forcing the discontinuance of Personal Surveillance Drones, the Langhorn/Davis Bill quietly slid through Congress. The Bill required every American Citizen to have a Federal Identification photo on file by the 4th of July, last year. In addition, every visitor to the country, every legal visitor, was required to present a photo ID upon arrival. A copy of that photo was immediately fed into the Federal Identification Photo File(FIPF) and became a permanent record therein. A second provision of the bill was the requirement that all businesses open to the public have a minimum of two security cameras in place within the same time frame. This meant any time, and every time, a person was exposed to a security camera his or her image went to Computer Central where the computer instantly matched it to that person's file photo. Supposedly, unless the subject had been "check loaded," once the person's identity was confirmed the image would immediately be deleted. Anytime a person who's photo had been check loaded ventured in front of a security camera, whether at a bank, or an airport, or a corner drug store, anytime such a person was photographed by a security camera, his or her location was immediately ascertained and appropriate action instigated. The ACLU had screamed. A few Democrat congressman, among them Senator Anderson, expressed concern; but most Americans agreed it was great for National Security. The Supreme Court upheld it, and Langhorn/Davis prevailed. The thing that made it all so ridiculous was the government's continuing refusal to seal the borders. Unphotographed "Illegal Aliens" still came and went, various states still complained, and Washington still turned a deaf ear to the situation.

The first problem Gunner had to face was where to go? Did he dare check into a hotel? He didn't think there was a hotel or motel in the country that didn't have a security camera watching the check-in desk. The visor on his Red Skins cap, pulled down low on his forehead, was probably all he needed to avoid computer recognition from cameras located above his head, but would do little good if he were to walk into one at eye level. It would be foolish for him to take chances. What he needed was a place where security cameras were not yet part of the operation. "Great idea, John," he told himself. "And just where would that be?"

Where indeed, he wondered. And by the way, just where the hell was he? He had no idea what bus he was on or where it was going. With all the thoughts that had been running through his mind it was not surprising he supposed, but it was pretty dumb. He turned his attention to the window and the world outside the bus. 31st Street NW, they were just passing 31st Street. Georgetown, he was in Georgetown. Something clicked in his mind. He had taped several stories at the historic Mount Zion

United Methodist Church on 29th Street, in Georgetown. One story was about the celebration of the church's 150th anniversary. The church had a history dating back to before the Civil War. The original building had actually served as a station on the "underground railway" helping escaped slaves reach freedom. The church was located in a mainly residential area and he remembered seeing one or two "Room for Rent" signs in nearby house windows. It would be highly unlikely for a private house, with a room or two available for rent, to have a security camera.

Georgetown Rooming House

"YESSS?" The woman looked at him questioningly.

"I saw the sign in your window," Gunner told her, "I'm looking for a room for a few days..."

"I only rent by the week," she told him. "Three hundred a week, paid in advance."

Gunner hesitated. He did not want to appear too eager, did not want to seem too well-off. "Is that the best you can do?" he asked after a moment.

"Yes," she told him. "You get a private bath room, TV, coffee and rolls in the morning and clean sheets once a week."

Gunner pursed his lips and looked away briefly. I'm counting my money and deciding if I can afford three hundred a week, he told himself. "All right," he said at last. "Can I see the room?"

The woman opened the door wider, "Come on in."

The room was in front, on the first floor. The "Room for Rent" sign was in its window. It was not large, but it looked clean and with windows on the side of the house as well as in front it would have good ventilation. He checked the bathroom: a stall shower, toilet and small basin; it too was clean.

"Okay." He nodded his head up and down as he reached into his pocket and pulled out a small roll of bills. "Can I move in now?"
"Soon as you pay the room is yours," she told him. "How long you 'spect to stay?"

He slowly counted out three fifties, six twenties, and six fives. "Just a week, I think. I'll know better in a day or so if that's okay."

"Yes. That's all right, you let me know if you want the room longer than a week and I leave the sign in the window. Somebody come wantin' the room I give you first refusal but then you got-a either pay for the next week or vacate when this week's up."

"Okay." Gunner said as he handed her the three hundred dollars.

"What's your name?" The question seemed an afterthought. Gunner didn't think she much cared what his name was.

"Bowen," he told her. "Don Bowen."

"All right Mr. Bowen. I'm Mrs. Aims. We like it to be quiet around here. No loud TV, 'specially after ten o'clock." She put the money in her apron pocket and started towards the door, then turned back. "Almost forgot. Here's your key to the front door." She held it out to him. "Room key's right there," she pointed to the door handle as she stepped into the hall and closed the door behind her.

Gunner sat down on the edge of the bed and tried to collect his thoughts. He believed he had "disappeared" as the colonel told him to. But now what? He had no idea. He gazed out through the gauze curtain covered window and wondered. Then it hit him! Senator Anderson. The man is in danger. What could he do? Could he do anything? Should he do anything? If the man was a traitor… No. No, there is no way Senator Orin Anderson could be a traitor. Something is terribly wrong. He had to warn the man. He needed to find a telephone, somewhere far away from here; somewhere safe.

Downtown Washington D. C.

A HUNDRED or so blocks away from his new home John Gunner got off the cross town bus and found a neighborhood saloon. "John's Tavern - Established 1946." A place that has been around this long might be just what the doctor ordered, he thought, it might very well be a place where security cameras were still mounted high above the heads of the patrons. Okay, nothing ventured nothing gained, he told himself. Pulling the visor of his cap down, he took his handkerchief out of his pocket as he entered, held it to his nose and contrived a sneeze. With his face thus partially covered he quickly looked around the room. High on the wall, opposite the entrance door a camera looked down at him. Lowering his head, he sneezed a second time as he made his way to the bar.

Pay phones being almost a thing of the past, he ordered a gin and tonic then held out a five dollar bill to the bar tender. "I need-a use a phone for a local call. I had a fight with my girlfriend. . ."

"Been there, done that," the bar tender laughed. Taking the fiver, he pointed with his chin towards the end of the bar, "Phone's down there. Tell her to come on over for a drink."

Looking down at his drink as he carried it to the phone, Gunner was careful not to expose more of himself than the top of his Red Skins cap to the second overhead camera covering the bar.

"Senator Anderson's office," a crisp female voice told him after the third ring.

"Chip Young, please Marina." Marina Morales was the receptionist in the senator's office. Gunner knew her casually.

"I'll see if he's in. May I tell him who's calling?"

For a second he wondered if he should give his name but Chip would not be likely to take a call from an unknown caller, "Yeah, this is John Gunner from TVNews."

"Oh. Hi Mr. Gunner, didn't recognize your voice. Just a second..."

Thirty seconds later Chip came on the line. "Hey John, what's up?"

"Listen, Chip. The senator is in danger, I can't go into it over the phone, we need to get together. Don't mention the name of the place but do you remember where we ran into each other a few days ago? You bought me a beer?"

"Yesss." Young's voice took on a questioning tone. "I remember the place." The inflection in Young's voice as he said "the place," told Gunner he did remember, the place was named "The Place."

"Chip, meet me there in half an hour and I'll give you all the information."

"John, John, I can't make it in half an hour, we have a committee hearing in fifteen minutes. What's this all about anyway? You say the senator is in danger? Why don't you come over here and talk to us?"

"I can't do that, Chip. It isn't safe for me and yes, the senator is in danger. This is serious, Chip. How soon can you meet me?"

"Jesus, I don't know. If it's that important, maybe five-thirty, six o'clock."

"All right, if that's as soon as you can make it. I just hope nothing happens to him before then."

National Airport - Washington DC

AIRPORTS were always crowded but Stephen Hunter believed none was ever as crowded as Washington National. Where did all the people come from he wondered. Removing his trade mark oversize horn rim glasses as moved down the jet-way into the terminal building, he replaced them with a rimless pair and became Richard Smith. He doubted very many people would recognize him as Stephen Hunter without the horn rims.

Large as the crowd was, it took only a moment for him to spot Paul Savage. By sheer coincidence Paul was already in DC when the order came through. Working with him always made assignments more easily accomplished and today's assignment was likely to be somewhat complicated.

Once Paul Savage knew Stephen had spotted him he walked slowly towards the exit doors. "He isn't 'Stephen'," Savage reminded himself, "Now he is Richard Smith." One of Hunter's many idiosyncrasies was his insistence that people always call him by his formal first name: Stephen or Richard, never Steve or Dick. The two had worked together on several assignments and enjoyed each others company. Hunter the art connoisseur, Savage the travel agent. A strange combination, but one that made moving about the world very much a non-suspicious part of their everyday life. Paul's main office and home was in Chicago, but Savage Travel's branch in DC did almost as much business as the Chicago office and it was Paul's practice to spend one week a month in Washington.

It wasn't until they reached Paul's car that the two spoke to each other. "Well well, Paul, definitely a non-attention getting vehicle," Hunter chuckled and reached to shake Savage's out stretched hand. "Good to see you."

"Hertz's least likely to be noticed," Savage grinned as he clicked the trunk open. "Isn't she a beauty?"

"Oh yes, I should say." Hunter/Smith placed his overnight case in the trunk, "I always think a slightly in need of a wash grey is all but invisible."

It wasn't until they were both seated in the car that Savage said, "We have a second assignment, Richard, it came through while you were in the air?"

"Really. A double header?"

"Not exactly. Two separate targets. The new one is for this afternoon.

Starbucks - 11th St. SE

GUNNER WONDERED if he was getting paranoid or was the enormity of the situation was just beginning to take hold? He really didn't know but, whatever the cause, he was becoming more and more cautious every moment. That was the reason he had decided to get here an hour early and not wait inside The Place for Chip Young. Instead, with cap brim carefully pulled down and handkerchief held to his nose, he had come to the Starbucks across the street, bought a Grande Latte and seated himself in the window where he could watch people coming and going. Where he could see Chip Young when he arrived, and be certain he was alone.

It was five-fifteen when he saw them. For some reason the car got his attention as it pulled to the curb not to drop off Chip Young, but a man and a woman. The car went on down the street, the couple went into The Place. Was it the kind of no frills government issue car? Was it the way the two were dressed? The way they carried themselves? Particularly the woman, there was just something about her. He didn't know what, but he was sure they were FBI, and some sixth sense told him they were looking for him. He realized he shouldn't be surprised. If someone were to call and say a senator is in danger who else would you contact? If he were Chip Young that is what he would have done. It was while he was considering this that a grey Ford sedan stopped in front of Starbucks to drop off a man; a man who looked very much like just about everybody else in the world except for one thing, he was carrying a still camera. A still camera just like the one in John Gunner's gym bag.

The man came towards Starbucks, walked up to an empty sidewalk table, tipped a chair forward, placed a newspaper on the table, then turned and came towards the entrance.

Probably because of the reflections in the window the man had not yet seen him, but as soon as he enters the building. . . The best thing Gunner could do would be nothing. Nothing that would call attention to himself. He found a piece of paper in his jacket pocket, an old grocery list he had long since forgotten was in there. Putting his right elbow on the table and resting his head on his hand he began to study the list while carefully, slowly, sliding his left hand over to the handle of his gym bag. The bag was heavy enough to be used as sort of a weapon if it came to that and, weapon or not, if he had to leave quickly it had to go with him. Everything he had was in that bag: fifty-five thousand dollars in cash, the still camera and a few clothes. The clothes he could replace, the money and the camera he could not.

Fortunately there was not the usual long line of people waiting to order and it was only a few moments before the barrista" called "Richard - Soy Latte," and the man, who seemed intent on watching the activity out on the street rather than inside the store, quickly picked up his coffee and hurried outside to the table he had selected without noticing John Gunner. As soon as the man settled down at his table Gunner casually stood up and walked slowly to the rear of the shop where the rest rooms were located, and where a back door led to the alley behind.

Stepping quickly into the alley Gunner carefully closed the door behind him then looked up and down the narrow street. Oh shit! Not fifty feet away, with its motor running, sat the grey Ford.. He could see the driver clearly. And the driver could see him. Panic! What to do?

There was an open door across the alley. Gunner ran to it and into the building. He slammed the door behind him, flipped the lock, then ran towards the front of the building. My God, he was in a beauty salon. Four women were seated in what he would call "barber's chairs," one female and two male beauticians were attending to them.

"What are you doing here?" One of the beauticians demanded. At almost the same time they heard a loud pounding on what Gunner knew was the back door he had just locked.

"Just passing through." he answered and ran as fast as he could to the front door and out onto 12th Street.

12th Street, South East

JOHN GUNNER would never again doubt the importance of good luck. 12th Street is "One Way" and not twenty feet from him, driver's side to the sidewalk, an older man was getting out of his car. Gunner ran up to the man, grabbed the car keys from his hand and, while pushing the man to the ground, told him, "I've got to take your car but I'll leave it where you can find it." Before the stunned man could do more than stare at him and shake his head, before any of the several people nearby could react, Gunner swung his bag into the car, jumped in, started it and took off.

As he pulled away from the curb, in the rear view mirror he could see the man with the camera rush out of the Beauty Salon's door. He could see one of the pedestrians helping the old man to his feet and pointing after him.

Two blocks down 12th Street traffic was stopped for a red light. In the mirror he could see the man with the camera jump into the grey Ford. Waiting for the light to change he watched as the Ford pulled away from the curb and cut dangerously into the fast lane.

The light changed. It seemed forever before the cars in front of him began to move while the cars in the lane next to him were racing past. In the mirror he watched the Ford as it gained several car lengths. It was no more than half a block behind when he came to a corner. The light there was changing… already red by the time he reached it. Ignoring a horn blast from the car he cut off Gunner made a right turn into the cross-street.

"Oh fuck!" he said out loud. The second car on the other side of the street was a police car. As he accelerated he saw the police car's flashers come on. Fortunately the car he had cut off was restricting traffic flow making it difficult for the police car to turn around and impossible for the Ford to follow. The block ahead was almost empty. He accelerated. At the next corner he made another screeching right turn. Half way down the block he spotted a parking garage. He could not see the police car or the grey Ford behind him. If luck was still with him they were still tangled up in traffic back on 12th Street. He pulled into the garage, snatched a ticket from the machine, then, as the gate swung open, he saw the flashing lights on the police car as it came round the corner behind him. Had they seen him entering the garage? Probably. He had only seconds to decide what to do next.

Turning up an exit ramp he stamped on the brake, switched off the engine, grabbed his gym bag and jumped out of the car. Snatching off his Red Skins cap, he ran ten yards up the exit ramp then stopped and turned to look back down the ramp. A policeman appeared at the bottom of the ramp. "Hey! Hey!" he shouted as he pointed towards the far side of the garage, "Son-of-a-bitch went that way." The policeman half waved at him then headed in the direction Gunner indicated. A moment later a car coming down the exit ramp skidded to a stop before bumping into the car Gunner had abandoned.

"What the hell's going on?" The driver shouted.

"Don't know," Gunner called back. "Cops are after somebody."

"Oh great." The driver shook his head. "How am I gonna get out-a here?"

"Yeah…" Gunner replied as he started up the ramp, "Me too."

Before he had taken more than another few steps a second car came down the ramp, stopped, and sound its horn. Looking towards this driver Gunner shook his head and shrugged his shoulders, then continued up the ramp. At the third level he made his way to the far side of the building where, as he expected, there was an exit stairway and windows along the side of the building giving him a view of the street below. No sign of the cop and the growing cacophony of car horns below suggested that at the moment the officer had more to be concerned with than ticketing a red-light cheating driver.

Resisting the temptation to run, Gunner slowly made his way down the exit stairs to the street door. Pushing it open, he started out onto the street. No, wait, be careful. The Ford, they could be out there looking for him, they could have turned down this street, they could be looking up and down any street. Carefully he leaned out from the garage doorway. He could see no sign of the Ford, nor any police activity. What he did see was a bus heading in his direction and a bus stop at the corner fifty yards away. Thank God for DC's public transportation system. One more look up and down the street. All clear. He ran to the corner arriving there just as the bus did. A moment later as the bus doors closed behind him, he felt safe at last Maybe not "safe," but definitely in less danger than he had been in a few minutes before.

Apartment C - 1147 Cherry Avenue

BERYL KINNEY closed her front door, kicked off her shoes, dumped the mail on her desk and headed for the kitchen. It was "that time" of the month, she was out of sorts, irritable and tired. What she needed was a glass of wine.

"Ahhh," she said out loud as she took the first sip. "That's better." After a second sip she carried her glass to the desk, sat down and looked at the mail she had dropped there. Nothing but junk! The ones addressed to "B. Kinney" were bad enough but the ones addressed only to "local resident" were really a nuisance. How does junk mail find you so quickly, she wondered.

An unexpected knock on her door surprised her. He didn't usually get home this early. She glanced out her window as she started towards the door. The TV van was not parked out front as usual, instead a grey Ford was parked where John usually found a spot. Wow, she thought, did he just blow some of that money. No, not our John Gunner she told herself as she opened the door expecting to see his smiling face… Only the knocking was not at her door, it turned out to be across the hall, at his door.

"Who are you?" She demanded. Strangers were not supposed to be in the hallway. Strangers were supposed to ring the entrance bell at the front door downstairs. "How did you get up here?"

The man looked startled as he turned to face her. "Oh, hello. Good evening. I'm a friend of John's. You haven't seen him have you?"

“Mr. Gunner is away. How did you get up here?” she asked again.

“John gave me a key,” he answered as he started for the stairs. “Sorry I disturbed you…”

The man disappeared down the stairway. Beryl closed her door and checked the lock. She did not believe John had given him a key. She went quickly to the window and watched the stranger climb into the grey Ford. As it pulled away she could not see if the driver was a man or a woman. It took her until almost midnight to compose a note to Aunt Sarah regarding the stranger in the hall, the slightly dirty grey Ford, and the fact that John Gunner had not come home.

Mrs. Aims House

BLINKING SLEEP from his eyes and feeling slightly disoriented, John Gunner found himself looking up at a strange ceiling. It wasn't like a sudden revelation, he knew where he was, it was just that it took his mind a second or two to catch up with itself. His wrist watch told him it was nearly nine o'clock and the daylight filling the room assured him it was nine o'clock in the morning, not nine at night. He couldn't remember the last time he had slept this late.

So what was he going to do with his first full day of disappearance? A shower and some clean clothes would be good for a start. Then, Mrs. Aims had mentioned coffee and rolls, if he weren't too late, that would hit the spot.

The water was hot and the shower was good. He toweled himself dry then decided to wash the underwear he had just taken off. That done, he stepped back into the bedroom, pulled on a clean pair of Tommy Hilfiger briefs and switched the TV on to the CNN News Channel he had located last night.

> *"A sad note at the top of our news today,"* the news anchor said slowly,
>
> *"Word has just reached us that Senator Orin Anderson died this morning of an apparent heart attack..."*

John Gunner did not hear the remainder of the news report.

NOT FAR from Georgetown a Private Telephone rang twice before being answered:

“Yes sir, good morning.”

“At least half the assignment went well,” an angry voice proclaimed.

“Yes, the other…”

“Unlike John Gunner,” the voice broke in, “Those two can be counted on to do whatever they’re told to do.”

“Yes sir, I’m certain of that.”

“And what about Gustafson?” The voice asked.

“Ummm. I think he is reliable.”

“You don’t sound all that confident.”

“Perhaps not. I’ll have a better feel for that once we clear up the Gunner matter.”

“And that better be damned soon!” The voice was angry again. “I don’t want all my plans fucked up Gordon!”

The connection was broken before a reply could be offered.

FBI Headquarters - Washington D.C.

JUST WHAT is it you're trying to tell me, Jane?" Special Agent David Christopher wanted to know.

"I'm not sure, sir." Agent Jane Shuman blinked her soft brown eyes twice, and took a slightly deeper breath than normal before continuing. She didn't want to make a fool of herself and she really had nothing to go on other than what she guessed was intuition; something pulling on a string somewhere in her mind, something telling her there was more to be learned. "But with Senator Anderson's death this morning," she continued, "… Well, I just keep thinking maybe there is more here than we realize."

"Run it past me again," her boss told her.

"Okay." The lifting of Jane's eyebrows was visible evidence of her frustration at being asked to tell him a lot of what he already knew. "A TVNews cameraman named John Gunner telephoned Senator Anderson's office yesterday afternoon. He spoke with Chip Young, the senator's chief of staff. He told Mr. Young the senator was in danger and asked Mr. Young to meet him at a restaurant named 'The Place.' Mr. Young suggested Mr. Gunner come to the office, he said he couldn't because he was in danger. Mr. Gunner had been in the senator's office earlier in the day to tape a statement the senator wanted to make but made no mention of any danger then. Mr. Young told him he could not meet with him until about five-thirty because he was going into a committee hearing with the senator. Mr. Gunner said okay, then Young telephoned us. Agent Winter and I went to intercept Mr. Gunner to find out what his call was all about. We arrived at The Place at approximately four-fifty, so we were certainly there in plenty of time. We stayed until six-thirty. Mr. Gunner never showed up. I telephoned the news desk at Mr. Gunner's office before we left, and again this morning. Nobody seems to know where he is.

"Umm-hmm." Special Agent Christopher made a slight throat clearing noise before continuing. Agent Shuman was a very pretty girl and almost young enough to be his daughter. Actually his oldest son was closer to her in age than he was and she was probably the smartest of the young agents working with him. Not only smart but intuitive. But he simply couldn't resist teasing her, just a little bit, from time to time. "Man doesn't show up for a beer," he said in a slightly condescending tone of voice, "That's pretty sinister all right. You think he may have had a premonition about Senator Anderson's heart attack?"

"I don't know Chris." Jane's patience level was being reached. "The man called Chip Young and told him the senator was in danger. I would just like to know what kind of danger he thought the senator was in and why he didn't show up for the meeting. I want to talk with somebody in charge of things over at TVNews and find out how I can contact the man and I want to see what he photographed in the senator's office." Now it was her turn to be condescending, "Can you go along with that?"

"I suppose…" Christopher's face broke into one of his occasional smiles. "Actually I'm rather surprised you waited this long to get started."

"Actually I didn't exactly wait, sir. After I checked Mr. Gunner's office again this morning I asked Norman, over at Computer Central, to Check Load him. Then I made an appointment to meet with his boss at eleven o'clock." It was Jane's turn to smile, "But, without an assignment, I thought I should get your approval to leave the building."

"Very good Agent Shuman, I love it when agents occasionally follow proper procedure." Christopher looked at his wrist watch. "You now have an assignment and according to my watch you are due there in less than half an hour." He glanced at Agent Shuman as she nodded in the affirmative, "In which case you better get off your …" Christopher made another slight throat clearing sound. "…<u>chair</u>, and be on your way."

"Yes sir." Agent Shuman rose gracefully from her chair and, with a slightly exaggerated sway to her hips as she turned, told him, "I'm off my… chair, and I will keep you advised Special Agent Christopher."

"That is the proper procedure Special Agent Shuman," David Christopher told her receding back.

"Piss-off Chris," she called over her shoulder while giving a slightly more exaggerated wiggle before breaking into a grin as she closed the office door behind her. The archaic FBI regulation requiring a door be left open when one male and one female were alone in an office always amused her.

TVNews.Gov Office

"THANK YOU for seeing me Mr. Gustafson."

"You are very welcome, Agent Shuman. Now have a seat. Let's have some coffee and a little less formality." Harry Gustafson pushed an empty cup towards the FBI agent then filled it with coffee from the carafe on his desk. "What is it you need from me?"

"Thank you sir," As she reached for the cup she noted the door to Gustafson's office was closed. Apparently Government protocol was not followed everywhere. Picking up the cup she took a sip before continuing. "I'm hoping you can give me a little information about one of your people, Mr. Gustafson." Damn! She said to herself. "information" was a very bad choice of words. Immediately she said it, she could see Gustafson's eyes flash.

"Information?" Gustafson sat up a little straighter. "I don't know why I should give you any information about my people."

"Yes sir. I mean, no sir. There isn't any reason why you should. That was a bad word. I'm not looking for information, I just want to contact Mr. John Gunner. The news desk people told me he has not been in the office since yesterday morning and is probably on a special assignment. They said you would be the only person who would know where I might reach him."

"All of which is true Agent Shuman, but isn't a reason why I should tell you."

“No sir, it surely isn’t.”

“Why do you want to get hold of John Gunner?” .

“I guess that’s the other side of the same coin, Mr. Gustafson, I can’t tell you that, it’s a confidential matter.”

“Okay Agent Shuman.” Harry Gustafson laughed as he pushed his chair back from his desk and started towards the door. “Next time maybe we can be more help to each other. Now you finish your coffee, I’ve got to go check the news room then I‘m going to lunch.”

“Yes sir, but before you go would it be possible for you to arrange for me to view Mr. Gunner’s coverage of Senator Anderson’s video statement the other morning.” Jane waited for a brief second or two before adding, “Or will it be necessary for me to get a warrant?”

“Ouch!” Gustafson stopped and turned back, “I guess it’s time to play hard ball, and I guess you should get a warrant Agent Shuman.”

“Yes sir, I can do that Mr. Gustafson. In fact,” Jane made a point of deliberately opening her note book, removing an official looking document and holding it out to Harry Gustafson, “I just happen to have one. Here you are.”

“Okay,” Harry knew when he was beaten, “I’ll set you up in a viewing room. Then, I’m going to lunch.”

“Thank you, sir.” Jane stood and followed Gustafson out the door.

Woodland Park Hotel - Washington, DC

THOUGHTS OF LUNCH and John Gunner were not exclusive to Harry Gustafson. Only a few blocks away, in the Oak Wood Room at the Woodland Park Hotel, similar thoughts were in the mind of Stephen Hunter as the wine steward hovered discretely behind his chair waiting for his reaction to the Petite Sarah he had just poured. Leaving his Richard Smith identity elsewhere, Hunter was a frequent guest at the Woodland Park where he was known as a good tipping well-to-do art dealer and man of exquisite taste. Lifting his glass towards the light coming through the nearby window Hunter looked through his trademark horn rim glasses at the warm, red color of the wine; swirled it around in the glass, then took a sip.

"Not bad Edmundo," Hunter said after a moment. He looked again at the color of the wine before taking a second sip, then, smiling up at the steward, he told the anxious man, "Really quite nice. You just may convert me,"

"Thank you, sir. Thank you." Mr. Hunter's satisfaction was very important. Edmundo knew Mr. Hunter preferred French wines but had been so impressed by this California vintage he asked him to experience it.

Actually not that good, Hunter told himself as the man filled his glass, but it isn't bad and it makes old Edmundo so happy. And it was time to be happy. After yesterday evening's fiasco at Starbucks, and encountering that woman at the target's apartment, this morning had gone very well. The constituent's breakfast had provided the perfect situation. There were at least seventy-five people in attendance and obviously not all were known to each other. Best of all it seemed that every other person there had a camera. Yes, the morning had gone well, now it was time to relax and enjoy a good lunch. He lifted the glass for another sip. Too bad Paul couldn't celebrate the morning's success with him but it was not a good idea for them to be seen together unless it was absolutely necessary, and never as Stephen Hunter.

Just thinking about being seen together made him uncomfortable, made him think about yesterday afternoon's adventures. Good God what had they been thinking of? Did they think they were in a movie car chase? What if they'd had an accident, or been arrested for a traffic violation? Fortunately there had been no such problems. The target got away, but that isn't our worry, he thought. It isn't our job to determine target and location, we are only required to go there and eliminate it. When somebody locates the target again we will deal with it. Meanwhile, here comes lunch. He glanced at his wrist watch, not quite one-thirty, ample time for a leisurely meal. His flight back to New York wasn't until four forty-five.

Senator Anderson's Office

"THANK YOU for seeing me, Mr. Young. I am anxious to talk with you but I didn't want to bother you on this terrible day. I know the senator's death must be a great shock."

Chip Young looked at the young woman whose hand he was shaking. Jesus, he thought, they get younger and younger. Special Agent Jane Shuman couldn't be thirty, yet here she was a full-fledged FBI Agent. And a damn good looking one too: slender, tall, probably five-eight or nine, nice figure, dark hair, no trace of grey, good jaw line, wide spread eyes, altogether a very attractive young woman.

"I don't know about shock," Young said slowly. "At least not yet, I don't think any of us really believe it yet. Shock will come when we realize he's actually gone." He gestured to the chair facing his desk, "Have a seat and tell me what's on your mind."

"Mr. Young, I want to get a bit more information about the phone call you received from John Gunner. We've been trying to contact him but no one seems to know where he is; or at least no one wants to tell us. His boss, Harold Gustafson, told me he is on an assignment, but he wouldn't give me any details."

"Really. That's kind of surprising." Young pushed his lips out and in, why should there be a problem contacting John, he wondered. "How can I help?"

"I just have a couple of questions if you don't mind…" Jane pulled a note pad from her shoulder bag and glanced at it. "You said Mr. Gunner called to tell you the senator was in danger and he wanted to meet with you to give you further information, is that right?"

"Yes, right."

"He also told you he could not come to your office because it would not be safe for him?"

"Yes again."

Jane made notes, then, "Mr. Gunner was one of the TV people who covered Senator Anderson's press conference yesterday morning?"

"Well it wasn't exactly a press conference, the senator just had a statement he wanted to put on the record, but yes, John was covering. He and Tom Wilson from the cable news network were the only two crews that showed up."

"Was that uncommon?"

"No," Young laughed. "Not at all. Sometimes TVNews is the only one covering such things. That's why the congress decided to finance 'em. Makes sure everybody can get something on tape for the folks back home. Means we can all be TV stars."

"I see…" Jane smiled. "Was there anything unusual about Mr. Gunner at that time?"

"Unusual? No… well, he did seem a little disconcerted; and he hurried out of the office when the senator finished. Said he had to run."

"Was that something strange?"

"Not really. Those news guys are on a pretty tight schedule sometimes."

"I understand." Jane made another note on her pad: "*Disconcerted.*" Young's statement coincided with her own supposition after viewing Gunner's video tape of the senator's statement. She had been somewhat surprised when the tape kept running after the senator left the podium - running until an off camera voice said, "You can turn off your camera now Johnnie."

"Now, may I ask what the senator spoke about?" She knew very well what the senator had said, she watched and listened to the video of him making the statement only a short time ago. But a lesson she had learned well was the need to get as many reports on, and comments about, an incident as possible. When these did not coincide, questions arose.

"Yeah, sure. I don't guess anybody thought it was very important, at least I haven't seen a mention of it on the news…" The expression on Chip Young's face as he spoke told Agent Shuman he was really surprised by the lack of media interest. "…What the senator said, umm… I've got a copy of his statement if you'd like it, anyway, basically what he talked about was the committee hearing that began yesterday afternoon. Orin believed big oil companies, particularly AllWorldOil, are financing the wars in the middle east in order to keep the oil supply limited and the price up. The hearing was originally scheduled for a month ago, Sheik al-Sameur was going to be our first witness, but, as you know, he died of a heart attack just after he arrived here in Washington."

"Yes, I remember," Jane said. Then, as an afterthought she asked, "Do you happen to know if Mr. Gunner covered the sheik's arrival?"

"No…" Young was obviously a bit surprised by the question. "I guess he might have, but I really don't know."

Another pause while Jane wrote some more in her notebook before asking, "The sheik's death was the reason the hearing was put off 'till now?"

"Right… Now with Orin's death…Lord knows when it will go on…if ever." Young leaned back in his chair and his eyes seemed to lose their focus as they looked away from her and she noticed tears in their corners. "It just seems so damn unbelievable that both men could die of heart attacks within less than a month of each other." Young took a handkerchief from his pocket and blew his nose. "I never had the slightest idea Orin had anything wrong with his heart."

Jane waited quietly for Chip Young to turn his attention back to her.

"Yes, well," his eyes re-focused on the FBI Agent. "Where were we?"

"The committee hearing; you were saying something about All World Oil and the fighting in the middle east," Jane prompted.

"Yes… I don't know where Orin was getting all his information from, he could be remarkably close mouthed about some things, but I know he was convinced AllWorld has a hand in what's going on over there."

"Oh my," Jane's reaction was one of seeming realization, "All World, isn't that the company the vice president brought to prominence?"

"Yes, indeed," Young agreed. Another pause, another tear, then: "What else can I tell you Agent Shuman?"

"Just a couple more things Mr. Young… You telephoned me," she glanced again at her notes, "At two-thirty, was that immediately after Mr. Gunner called you?"

"Nooo…" Young cocked his head. "No, I guess it was maybe a half hour or so later. The senator and I were on our way to the hearing when he called, it wasn't until we were settled in the hearing room that I thought to contact you people."

“So his call to you would have been at about two o’clock, give or take a few minutes?”

“Yeah. That would be about right.”

“And you haven’t heard anything from Mr. Gunner since that call? He wasn‘t at the constituents breakfast by any chance was he?”

“No, no, he certainly wasn’t, and no, I haven’t heard from him.”

“Mr. Young, did anyone else know about the meeting Mr. Gunner wanted? Did you discuss it with anyone?”

“No…” Young twisted his head slightly before adding, “I don’t believe so.“

“Could anyone have overheard your call to us?”

Young thought for a moment before answering. “I suppose so. Gordon Wolfe was sitting right next to me… so was Eric Fallon from Senator Stones’ office.”

Jane made one more notation on her pad, then got to her feet. “Thank you for taking all this time with me, Mr. Young. My sincerest condolences on the senator’s death. I’ll try not to bother you anymore,” She placed a business card on Young’s desk, “I’ll appreciate it if you let me know if you hear from Mr. Gunner again.”

“Yes, yes, of course, I’ll do that. And I will appreciate it if you let me know what John has to say when you find him.”

1147 Cherry Avenue

THE FIVE MINUTE WALK from the bus stop to her apartment building gave Beryl Kinney ample time to re-think her plan. There was no reason it shouldn't work. If he was coming home at all he never got there before six o'clock, and it was now only five. Still, she would be careful.

The big front door opened easily and locked automatically behind her while she half ran up the stairs to her apartment and telephoned John Gunner. After four rings his voice announced, "Hi. Off getting the news, leave a message." She waited for two minutes, then called again. Same result: the answer machine. Convinced he was not at home she walked across the hall to his door. If it turned out he was home, she was preparing dinner; would he like some? She knocked, waited, knocked again, then used her "openall" key to let herself in.

"Hi fish. Nobody home, eh?"

An hour later Aunt Sarah received a coded message:

Subject no-show.
Cash, Helms ID,
some clothing missing.
Will Eschelon Helms.

Beryl believed if John Gunner was going to travel very far, sooner or later he would use his Albert Helms ID, then Eschelon would let her know when, and where, and why.

In spite of her training in computer technology Eschelon's ability to examine all electronic transmissions and pick out specific phrases, words, or names still amazed her. Once Albert Helms' name and address was entered into the system it would seek out and register every electronic transmission of that name, but would only report such transmissions when the name was somehow combined with part of, if not all, the Staten Island address.

Needwood Lake, Rock Creek Park

SEVEN O'CLOCK in the morning is really a lovely time of day, John Gunner thought. Especially here in the park. The sun was just high enough to cast bright golden beams of light down through the new leaves on the trees. Out on the lake a gentle breeze was making slight ripples in the water and all sorts of birds were chirping happily in the woods. It was hard to believe such a bucolic setting could exist practically in the middle of a city, only a few miles from the White House, only a few miles from the capital. After spending most of yesterday hidden away in a movie theatre he was delighted to be outdoors in the fresh air.

Gunner knew the colonel would be along in less than five minutes. The colonel was an absolute fanatic about keeping to a schedule. Here behind this large rock just a few feet off the trail, bent over tying and re-tying his shoe laces, was the perfect place to wait. The rock itself was hardly visible through the spruce trees and vines, standing behind it he would be completely hidden from anyone coming up the trail until he was certain it was the colonel and that he was alone. He looked up from his shoelaces as he heard approaching footsteps. It could be anybody but somehow he knew it was the colonel. He waited for him to pass, then stepped out and fell in behind. "Good morning, Sir."

If his greeting surprised the colonel he didn't show it, he didn't turn his head, nor miss a step. "Hello John." He made a gesture with his hand, "Come up alongside."

Gunner fell in next to the colonel, who's pace was steady but not fast, then asked, "Was the senator really an enemy?"

"That is a very inappropriate question, John."
"Yes sir, but…"

"No 'buts', John! Questioning an order is disobedience. Refusing to obey an order is desertion!" The colonel took a few more strides before continuing in a softer tone of voice, "I realize your failure was not deliberate. I know you are a loyal agent. But you have put yourself in a hell of spot my boy. If I can do anything to straighten this out I will, but right now I don't know how. Right now you need to get away from me and get away from DC to someplace where no one can find you. Washington is not safe for you John, there are two agents looking for you." He glanced at Gunner before continuing, "Call me from a secure phone in a couple of days."

"Yes sir. But who are 'they' sir?"

"John." The colonel's voice again took on a stern tone. "You know I can't tell you that."

"I understand." Gunner's tone of voice belied his statement. "Anyway, I saw both of them the other day."

"You did?" The colonel's surprise was obvious. "Well try not to see them again. Call me in a couple of days but right now beat it out of here because Larry's waiting for me just beyond the turn up there. . ."

Gunner looked up the trail. Perhaps two hundred yards ahead it began to bend away from the lake shore and into a parking area. "Larry," Gunner knew, was Larry Gold, the colonel's driver.

"If Larry sees you and me together…" The colonel let his sentence hang for a moment, before adding, "I think you know that might not be good."

Gunner stopped running, the colonel continued on. "Thank you, sir," he called after him. "I'll call you…" he added.

Mrs. Aims' House

"MRS. AIMS," Gunner wrote on the white paper drug store bag the shaving gear he bought at Walgreens came in, *"I think I have a job in Arlington. If I'm not back by day after tomorrow it means I don't need the room anymore. Thanks for everything."* He signed it *"D. Bowen,"* then went into the bathroom and carefully shaved off the beard he had been nurturing for the past ten months. His latest Press Pass photo had been taken with the beard, maybe removing it would slow down Computer Central recognition. Probably not, but anything was worth trying. He was ready to disappear.

"Disappearing," in his mind at least, meant getting out of town. How best to do that had required some serious thinking. Security at air terminals made plane travel impossible, and security at train stations was almost as tough, but bus stations were a little less efficient. Ever since he had done the stories about Security Central he had been a curious observer of security camera placement where ever he went. He and Beryl had taken the bus up to Baltimore to go to a ball game just a few days ago and, if he remembered correctly, the cameras at the Greyhound Terminal were high overhead. Without a beard, wearing his Red Skins cap with the bill pulled down and sneezing into his handkerchief, he thought he would be safe.

Greyhound Bus Terminal

SETTLING BACK in his seat, Gunner checked his wrist watch: almost noon. They were not scheduled to leave for another ten minutes but the bus was already more than half full. As he had hoped, things in the terminal had gone smoothly. They had not asked for anything more than his name. They didn't ask to see any ID, and paying cash for the ticket had not raised any eyebrows. But even a bus ticket could leave traces. For instance, a one-way ticket might raise an eyebrow. How many one-way tickets would they sell in a two day period? How difficult would it be to run a check on each one? So, the answer to that had been simple, he used the name Jim Woolley and bought a round trip ticket to a place where a lot of other people were always going, Atlantic City.

Atlantic City was not a place Gunner cared for. To him it represented the ultimate example of "haves and have-nots." Along The Boardwalk, facing the ocean, huge hotels stood shoulder to shoulder. Inside, softly lit lavish gold and silver casinos dominated acres of maroon carpeted floors. Minimum bets seemed to be $25 or $50 and rooms were $300, $400, $500 a night and more. Truly a world for High-Rollers. But just behind the grand hotels, only a block away from the ocean, Atlantic City looked very much like a slum. The streets were lined with rows of older two and three story wooden buildings, most of them needing paint, and it always seemed street sweepers had ignored the area for many days. Maybe not a "slum," John decided, but very definitely run down, definitely a world of people whose weekly incomes probably did not equal the cost of one night in a hotel room only a few hundred feet away.

Atlantic City, New Jersey

STEPPING OFF THE BUS Gunner felt confident he had "disappeared" from DC, and he was not supposed to call the colonel for another day at the earliest, so he might as well stay in Atlantic City but it was certainly not where he wanted to spend any more time than necessary. His experience with a rooming house in DC had been a good one and seemed to be the right idea for Atlantic City too. After walking up and down several streets finally on Baltic Avenue, just a block off Martin Luther King Highway, he found a large wood frame house with a "Room for Rent" sign in a front window. The building was old but the second floor room was reasonably clean. It had a shower, a TV set and a twin size bed, the rent was only two hundred a week, half of what a hotel room a block away would cost for one night. What more could he ask? Well, for one thing, he could ask for a better way to carry his money than having it stuffed into his gym bag. He needed to find a way to convert his money into traveler's checks, or bank checks, or something he could carry more easily. Here in Atlantic City, where a lot of cash money changed hands, there should be little or no problem buying checks of one kind or another. He would buy them using the name on his fake driver's license: Albert Helms, Staten Island, NY. The problem might come at the other end, the cashing them in end. Would his fake ID hold up? Would his "disguise" be good enough to fool bank cameras? Bank cameras would undoubtedly be far better quality than the old units in the bus terminal. He would have to be careful. He would check a couple of banks in the morning.

TVNews.Gov Office

"CALL ON LINE THREE," the voice coming over the intercom announced. Picking up the phone the colonel answered, "Harry Gustafson…"

"Good morning Mr. Gustafson, my name is Beryl Kinney," a slightly exasperated sounding woman told him. "I'm a friend of John Gunner's and I'm wondering if there isn't somebody there who can tell me where he is and when he will be back?"

An alarm bell sounded in Gustafson's head the moment she spoke Gunner's name. Friend? What friend? Be careful, he told himself. "I'm sorry Miss Kinney," he said slowly. "What is it you're asking?"

"I'm asking about John Gunner. I know he gets sent off on assignments from time to time, but we had a date for last night and I haven't heard from him in three days, so I'm wondering if he is alright."

"Oh yes, John's fine. He is off on an assignment and probably pretty busy. Sorry he didn't let you know. I'm sure he'll be in touch as soon as he finds time."

"Can you tell me where he is? How I can contact him?"

"I'm sorry Miss Kinney, it's against our policy to give out that kind of information but don't worry, John's fine. I'm sure you'll hear from him soon." Gustafson hung up the phone without waiting for her to say more. "Oh Shit!" he said out loud. Where in the world did she come from? Who the hell is she? How in

Christ's name does she know John? How does John know her? Is this something I should report? He wondered. Of course it is but, God knows, John's in enough trouble already. Adding a curious female to the mix would only make it worse. A lot worse. Better say nothing until I can talk to him and find out who she is and what's going on.

Atlantic City, NJ

THE LONG BILL on John Gunner's new fishing cap did an excellent job hiding his face from overhead cameras, unfortunately it did an equally good job of blocking his view of things above his head; in this case it was the discreet sign in a third floor window of the Bank of America building he was entering. A sign that read: **Federal Bureau of Investigation.**

As he hoped would be the case at lunch hour, the Bank of America was very busy. Head down, fisherman's cap in place, reading a newspaper, Gunner waited patiently in the third of five lines while a courteous but somewhat overworked teller took care of the half dozen customers ahead of him. It wasn't until he stepped up to the window and asked about Traveler's Checks that he panicked. At eye level, six feet behind the teller, a security camera was looking directly at him.

"Sir," Gunner realized the teller was speaking to him. "We offer Traveler's Checks in denominations from twenty dollars up to one thousand dollars. What would you like?"

"Gee," John lowered his head and looked down at his wrist watch. "I didn't realize how late it is. I'm sorry, I have an appointment. I'll have to come back later."

"Yes sir," the teller called after him as he turned away. "Have a nice day."

Two floors above a light was flashing on the main computer. A flashing light and a picture of John Gunner together with information as to where he had been detected by Security Central was being displayed. One of the newer features of the Security Central computer system was its ability not only to identify search subjects but instantly advise the FBI office nearest to the subject's location. "Jesus Christ!" Special Agent Frank O'Connell exclaimed. "He's right downstairs…in the bank!"

Had Agent O'Connell been in a bit less hurry he might have realized the man he brushed against as he ran towards the bank entrance, the man in the dark blue fisherman's cap, was the man who's picture was displayed on the screen he clutched in his hand, the picture he moments later showed to the teller in window three as he asked if she recognized him.

Greyhound Bus # 8705

LESS THAN AN HOUR after leaving the Bank of America, John Gunner placed his now half empty gym bag in the overhead rack then settled himself into a window seat. The bus was going to Philadelphia. He had no particular reason for going to Philadelphia, the bus just happened to be the first bus scheduled to depart when he arrived at the terminal.

After dashing out of the Bank of America he had slowly regained his poise and his brain began to function again. Obviously he could not be certain his picture had been check loaded but he knew damn well he better act as though it had been and he must assume the Central Computer had identified him. Therefore he must assume they knew he was in Atlantic City. Locating him in Atlantic City might be difficult but even with the odds in his favor it did not seem like a good chance to take. Better, he decided, he should get out of town fast, before they had time to organize check points. It seemed obvious the best way to do that was the same way he got there, by bus. There were not many cameras located in the Atlantic City bus terminal and they were not as strategically placed as they might be.

Thinking of strategic camera placement caused a chill to run up his spine. He really had been surprised by the camera at the bank. Jesus, it was right in his face! Well, whether the bus terminal had good camera placement or not, he had quickly decided to find a bit more camouflage before going there. On his way to the bank he had stopped at the large Rexal Drugstore on Martin Luther King Highway where he bought the fisherman's cap and sun glasses he wore into the bank. Remembering that like most drug stores it was crammed with everything other than drugs he returned there and in no time found everything he needed: A wide brim rain hat to replace the fisherman‘s cap, and a loose fitting rain coat. There had been showers in the morning and the weather was uncertain so a rain outfit wouldn't seem conspicuous or out of place. Best of all, a money belt. Why hadn‘t he thought of it before? He didn't need travelers checks, he hadn't needed to go to the bank, a money belt was the answer. A simple money belt able to hold most of the bills that had been riding in his gym bag. The rain coat hid the bulge of the belt around his waist, and the rain hat brim was wide enough to block his face from any camera that was placed higher than his head. Final item, the drug store photo department provided him with a case that would hang around his neck and carry his still camera. Feeling secure with these precautions he bought a round trip ticket, boarded the bus and now, waiting for departure, he was trying to relax.

An hour and a half later John Gunner stepped outside the Philadelphia bus terminal and looked down the street stretching out before him. He had been in Philadelphia before but not overnight and he had no idea where to stay. Before finding a place he wanted to contact the colonel. There were four pay phones mounted on the wall just outside the terminal doors. If there were security cameras watching the area he had not spotted them and even if there were, he was confident the rain hat would conceal his identity.

Washington, DC

HARRY GUSTAFSON grimaced as he listened to the angry voice in his ear, "Do I understand you would compromise the unit in order to protect this man?"

"No, no, of course not," Gustafson shook his head, "I am simply asking you to reconsider the matter. John Gunner is one of our best people. We simply cannot afford to eliminate him."

"'Best people' do not warm the enemy and do not desert," the angry voice said softly. "However if you believe it is necessary to talk further about it come over here in the morning and we'll have breakfast."

"What time?"

"Eight-thirty."

The phone went dead as Gustafson was saying, "Thank you." He knew tomorrow's breakfast meeting would be his last chance to save the young man he had come to think of almost as a son.

Moments later the private phone rang again. Gustafson rolled his eyes upward as he reached for the instrument. Probably calling to change plans, he thought. But it wasn't a change in plans, it was John Gunner.

"Hello Harry." Gunner did not identify himself. He knew the colonel would recognize his voice and knew the use of his name could possibly cause a problem.

“Who is Beryl Kinney?” Harry asked without preamble.

“Beryl?...” The colonel’s question caught him very much by surprise.

“Yes, John. Who the hell is Beryl Kinney?”

“She… she’s a girl I met.” Gunner answered slowly. “She lives across the hall from me.”

“Across the hall since when?” the colonel asked.

“A couple of months ago…”

“And you haven’t told me anything about her.” The disappointment in Gustafson’s voice was obvious. “Jesus John, you have an unbelievable ability to dig a deeper hole for yourself.”

Gunner could not think of a response. After a moment the colonel continued: “John, I have a breakfast meeting scheduled in the morning. I’ll try to get things straightened out, meanwhile stay hidden, stay out of trouble, and for Christ sake don’t pick up any more stray women. Call me tomorrow,” he added before switching off.

FBI Headquarters

"WELL JANE, was it Gunner or wasn't it?" Special Agent David Christopher wanted to know. When it was time for business, David Christopher was all business, and now was that time.

"I'm certain it was," she answered. "I looked at the security camera picture and the ID photo, I have no doubt it's the same man."

"And what have the people in Atlantic City come up with?" He asked.

"Not much so far," she grimaced. "The bank teller thought the man she talked to was Gunner, but she had no idea where he came from or where he was going. Our people are working on it but God knows how many hotel rooms there are in AC, it's a bit like looking for a needle in a hay stack. Anyway, my guess is he realized he was on candid camera and couldn't wait to get out of town. My bet is he's on a bus right now. You know there are busses coming and going every few minutes in Atlantic City and the camera coverage in bus terminals isn't all it could be."

"You're probably right." Chris agreed. Jane's feeling something was not quite as it should be when John Gunner did not shown up for his meeting with Chip Young seemed fully vindicated. The man is obviously on the run, Chris thought. She had made a smart move putting him on the check list.

Right or wrong," Jane continued, "I would like to have another talk with Harry Gustafson."

“Good idea,” Chris agreed. “Maybe this time we should invite him to come down here.”

“I’ll get right on it.”

Christopher’s phone rang as Jane got to her feet and started towards the open door. “Hang on,” he called after her, “Phone’s for you.”

“Agent Schuman,” she told the instrument then listened to a brief message. “Thank you, I’ll be right there.”

She handed the phone back to her boss. “That was Norman, they just made a match for Gunner at the bus terminal in Philadelphia. I want to see it, and Chris, if it looks solid I want to go up to Philly…”

“Go ahead. We’ll wait ’till you get back to call Gustafson.”

Philadelphia, PA.

TWO BLOCKS down Filbert Street John Gunner found The Palms. Just why anyone would name a hotel two blocks away from the bus terminal in Philadelphia "The Palms" was far beyond his comprehension, but there it was, in all its seedy glory, complete with a broken letter "a" in the electric sign above the entrance. A place this crumby is not likely to have much of a security system, he told himself as he pulled his rain hat down over his forehead and climbed the stairway to the hotel lobby one flight above a beauty parlor.

The Palms lobby, no bigger than the bus he had ridden in from Atlantic City, boasted a six foot high, genuine fake palm tree as it's center piece and main décor. "Okay," Gunner said to himself as he spotted a security camera high above the reception desk, "They got a palm tree."

The room rate was $49, cash, credit cards were not accepted and registration required only a name and a general address. "Sign here please," the clerk directed him as he pointed to the registration sheet.

"Martin Fields" came to Gunner's mind, "New York City."

"Thank you Mr. Fields."

"Thank you," Gunner replied as he accepted the room key.

"You're quite welcome," the clerk smiled and pointed to the stairs. "Two flights up, 4th floor, down the hall, 403, on the right hand side."

Interesting man, the clerk. A days growth of beard on his face, wearing jeans and an old tee shirt, but something about him, his manner and voice pattern, Gunner thought indicated a measure of education and sophistication totally out of balance with the look, the clothes, and the hotel.

The room was much better than Gunner expected. The bed seemed comfortable and the sheets were spotlessly clean. The bathroom: a small shower, basin and toilet in a space no larger than a closet, was also clean and odor free. "Pretty damn good for forty-nine bucks," he told himself as he switched on the TV set and settled into the one chair in the room. Time for the five o'clock news.

Nothing new. The wars in Syria, Pakistan and Afghanistan were still dragging on; suicide bombers were still at work; Arab civilians were still bending over broken and bleeding bodies; US troops were still banging open wooden doors to falling down buildings. He wondered how soon someone would be banging down the door to a room he was in.

He slept well. The bed was comfortable and his morning shower was great. He toweled himself dry then switched on the 8AM news. It was almost the same as last night: another skirmish along the Pakistan/Afghanistan border, only three American Advisors killed. Only three Americans killed… He shook his head as he pulled on his Hilfiger briefs. How could the newscaster brush it off so lightly? Three more bodies to send back home; three more American families destroyed. Three more to add to the total. What was it now? Well over fifty thousand since this never ending war began. There must be some way to stop it. He had hoped, he had believed, he could help. Could get rid of some of those blood thirsty terrorists. He had tried to do his part, until Senator Anderson.

He sat down on the bed with a sock in one hand. Why a United States Senator? Well Jesus, he told himself, I'm not supposed to know the whys and wherefores. I'm a soldier in the ranks. I'm supposed to obey orders. And I didn't. Obviously Anderson was a traitor, otherwise he would not have been eliminated. My job. my duty, was to carry out my orders. I didn't, and now there is an order out on me. G1 is looking for me, and so is the FBI. At least I think it's the FBI, and that has to be because I called Chip Young. Why the hell did I do that?

He sat gazing at the wall, not really seeing anything, just thinking for many seconds. How could he ever prove his loyalty after making that call to Chip Young? His best hope was Colonel Gustafson. His only hope was Colonel Gustafson. That thought brought him back to action. He looked at his wrist watch, nearly 8:30. He should get some breakfast then telephone the colonel. And he should do that from some place far away from the bus terminal and The Palms.

It looked like sunshine angling down the air shaft outside his window, in any case it wasn't raining, and that meant it might be a good day for a run. He loved to run and he needed exercise. He pulled on his running shorts, his Reeboks and a loose fitting sweat shirt that would cover the money belt. Running would be a good way to get somewhere without taking a bus. Remembering the need for caution, he grabbed the old Red Skins cap out of his bag and pulled it down low on his forehead before leaving the room.

The same room clerk who had been on duty when he checked in last night was behind the desk this morning. He smiled as Gunner approached him, "Good morning Mr. Fields."

"Good morning yourself and if you call me Marty I'll know you're talking to me, not my farther.

"Fair enough, Marty." The clerk stuck his hand out, "I'm Lucas."

"Hi Lucas." Gunner dropped his gym bag on the floor and shook the man's hand. "Now we're on a first name basis I wonder if I can ask a favor?"

“You can ask,” Lucas laughed. “That does not mean it will be granted.”

“Understood.” Gunner reached down and picked up his bag. “Favor is, could you keep an eye on this bag for me while I’m out. I’m always nervous about leaving things in a hotel room.”

“Favor granted,” the clerk grinned at him. “Baggage watching is one of the many services provided by The Palms.” He reached out to take the bag. “You want to leave the camera too?”

“No, thanks. I’m gonna do a little jogging and a little site seeing. Maybe take a picture or two.”

“Sounds like an exhilarating morning,” Lucas put the bag down behind the desk. “I’m on ’till seven tonight. If you’re not back by then I’ll put your name on it and lock it in the office. Benny, the night man, will get it for you.”

Turning north as he left the hotel Gunner headed up Filbert Street until reaching Arch Street where he turned east, toward the river. Running with a bulging money belt around his waist and a camera hanging from his neck was not really possible but he managed a reasonable jogging stride which was giving him more exercise than he’d had in a couple of days. At the end of Arch Street he found a road running south, past the docks. If the road had a name he did not see it, nor could he see very much of the river either, just occasional glimpses between the side by side pier buildings. Rivers were supposed to be beautiful, he thought, but obviously not the Delaware River, at least not while it is part of the city’s commercial waterfront.

Washington, DC

UNDER NORMAL circumstances Harry Gustafson would have found an opportunity to have breakfast in the Woodland Park Hotel's Oak Room most delightful, however this morning's breakfast was far from that. They sat quietly until the waiter was out of ear shot, then, "When did he tell you about this woman, Harry?"

"When I talked with him yesterday," Gustafson answered.

"Harry, I cannot believe this. You talked with Gunner yesterday and you did not report it; you learned of this woman and did not report that either?…" A pause, a sip of coffee, a shake of the head, then very softly, "You realize this practically makes you an accomplice…."

"Oh Jesus, don't you understand? John Gunner is as loyal and dedicated as any member of this unit. He has done outstanding work! He was simply incapable of eliminating a United States Senator. He blacked out." Gustafson took a deep breath, "I'm not sure I could have done it either," he said slowly. "It just doesn't seem to fit the mission we were given…"

"Determining our missions is not your responsibility Harry. The order on John Gunner stands; and I will look into this Kinney woman at once."

National Security Administration Headquarters

"IMMEDIATE ACTION" requests were not often received by NSA Research Analyst Martin Small. A member of the large unit charged with reading and evaluating individual electronic correspondences between people in the United States and people in other countries, Annalist Small's tiny piece of the huge pie was correspondence with Spain and Portugal. His job was normally one of slow, some would say "tedious," repetition. Only twice in the three years he had been so engaged had he found anything even remotely suspicious. Each was later determined to be nothing, but Annalist Small's appreciation for the importance of his job as a protector of national security was so strong that his devotion to it never wavered. Not surprisingly, therefore, today's "Immediate Action" request, un-nerving though it was, brought forth a flurry of activity. In very short order, from the file of literally millions of recorded out of the country communications stored in the massive NSA computer, he had produced and studied a total of six subject messages. Now he was ready to prepare his report:

"Beryl Kinney is a computer technician at Federal Aviation Administration. Duration of employment, one and one-half years: New York City fifteen months, transferred to DC March 1st this year." Small spoke clearly, carefully into his microphone. *"Subject has exchanged six messages with 'Aunt Sarah" in Madrid, Spain. Messages indicate Aunt Sarah is not actually family member but tour guide whom Kenny met while vacationing Spain prior to moving to Washington, DC. Nothing*

in messages considered unusual or suspicious. There is no indicated threat level."

Annalist Small returned the microphone to its holder and pressed the "Transcribe" button, it would be on his section chief's desk in less than two minutes. He hoped she would be aware of his very prompt and efficient response to her "Immediate Action" order.

Philadelphia, PA

AFTER RUNNING for nearly an hour, jogging really, John Gunner rounded a bend in the un-named road and found himself looking at a large parking area filled with trucks surrounding a diner named "Bill Clinton's Trucker's Lounge." He chuckled and wondered if the former president had ever eaten there. Probably not, but he was hungry and where would he find a better place than this, he asked himself.

Inside, Bill Clinton's looked like every other diner he had ever seen: long and narrow; on one side a counter stretching the full length of the room with backless stools facing the open pass-through windows into the kitchen; along the other side Formica tables and chairs.

Security cameras? At least four he could see, mounted high on the wall behind the counter. The handkerchief he was using to wipe sweat from his forehead and the bill of his cap would protect him from them.

Three waitresses were busy hustling plates of food to a crowd of would be diners. "Seat at the counter," one called to him.

Checking the angle of his cap he looked in the direction she had indicated and made his way to the empty stool. As he sat down another waitress asked if he wanted coffee as she placed a plate of food in front of the man seated next to him. He told her "Yes," then looked toward the man she had just served. His breakfast consisted of three fried eggs, a large portion of cottage potatoes, six strips of bacon, several slices of tomato and three pieces of toast. "Doesn't look like you go out-a here hungry."

"Sure don't," the man laughed as he shook pepper over everything on his plate. "I ain't seen you around here before," he glanced down at Gunner's running shorts, "You don't look like no trucker neither."

"No," Gunner answered. "Just out for some exercise, saw the sign and figured it might be a good place to eat."

"The best." The man shoveled a large fork full of cottage fries into his mouth. "Mary'll fix ya up," he nodded towards the waitress who was pouring coffee into Gunner's cup, "She's the best."

"Know what-chu want?" Mary asked.

"Yeah," Gunner answered. "I'd like what he's got only about half as much."

"Ain't got no half eggs," she laughed, "Outside-a that I can pretty much do it."

"Sounds good," Gunner told her.

Fifteen minutes later Gunner used his last piece of toast to mop up the remaining egg yolk, swallowed the last of his third coffee re-fill, took a deep breath, and headed for the payphones he had seen next to the front entrance when he came in. It was twenty minutes to ten, the colonel should be back from his breakfast meeting by now.

Washington, DC

HAVING WALKED the three or so miles from the Woodland Park back to his office Harry Gustafson sat down behind his desk and put his head in hands. The walk had done little to help him regain his composure. John Gunner was the son he almost had; the son Mary Lou was carrying when the bomb went off; when the embassy walls collapsed; when the war became very personal. Now his own country wanted to take the life of the young man who somehow had become that son. The situation was intolerable! But intolerable or not, there was no one else to turn to, no one else who could rescind the order on John.... Well, that was not true. . . G1 is the president's responsibility. The president may have delegated that responsibility, none the less it is still the president's, so it is to the president he must turn. And if the suspicion growing in his mind was even partially correct, if G1's mission has been corrupted, only the president could correct the situation. Years in the military had instilled in Harry Gustafson the need to properly follow the chain of command. To go over the head of a senior officer... to seek an audience with the Commander in Chief... It was against all his training. But he must. It is the only way he could save John Gunner.

Moments later his thoughts were interrupted by Gunner's phone call. "Good morning sir," John's familiar voice sounded in his ear. "Hope I'm not calling too early."

"No. No, not too early." Gustafson hesitated for a moment before continuing. "John the meeting did not go well. I have another direction to go in but it may take me a while. In the meantime..." The colonel paused. Gunner could hear him taking a deep breath followed by a soft sigh. "...In the meantime you need to get truly lost. Get some throw away cell phones then go far away and call me tomorrow afternoon."

"Yes sir."

Philadelphia, PA

IT WAS ALMOST noon when Gunner arrived back at The Palms and climbed the steps up to the hotel lobby.

"Hi Marty," Lucas called as he reached down behind the desk for Gunner's bag. "Two people were looking for you while you were out." He handed the bag to Gunner. "At least the picture they showed me might have been you. They were FBI looking for a man named John Gunner. Said they were checking all hotels near the bus terminal and took a quick look at the register...

"Gunner lifted his bag off the counter and held his breath as he waited for Lucas to say more. "...I told them we don't have anyone registered here under that name and the man in the picture didn't look like anyone I know."

Gunner exhaled.

"One of them left a card," Lucas picked up a business card and held it out for Gunner to see. "Special Agent Jane Shuman. She said if this guy should turn up they would appreciate a call, told me thanks and left."

"I owe you one, Lucas."

"Not really," Lucas said slowly. :Some years back the Feds and I had a bit of a disagreement. Agent Shuman and her partner seemed like nice people but I have no great love for the FBI.

"Whatever the reason, I owe you..." Gunner took another deep breath before adding, "I'm gonna take a quick shower then clear out of here, but I'd like to stay registered in the room for tonight if that's okay." Flashing a big smile Lucas told him, "There is nothing we like better here at The Palms than having rooms paid for and not used."

Pulling a small roll of bills from his pocket Gunner counted out forty-nine dollars. "Here's for tonight then," he said slowly. "And thanks, Lucas. I'll never be able to pay you back, but I won't forget you."

"Go take your shower," Lucas laughed, "Before I begin to cry." As Gunner started to turn and head for the stairs Lucas added, "Wait a second… 403 has been made up. Since you didn't leave anything in that room, why don't you use 314." He held out a key. "314 is right next to the fire stairs. I'll give you a ring if I think there's any reason you might want to use them. I'll leave you registered in 403."

After taking what, for him, was a prolonged shower, Gunner dressed then stuffed his still sweaty running clothes into the gym bag. The only way the FBI could have found him in Philly was a security camera at the bus station. He thought he had been careful enough; obviously he hadn't. He needed to get away from Philadelphia quickly without seeing any more security cameras. Half way out the door he stopped, turned back, took a $100 bill from his money belt and put it on the bed. He picked up the room phone and waited for Lucas to answer.

"Lucas, just for fun I think I'll use the fire stairs. Can you come up here and pick up something I'm leaving on the bed? I don't want anyone else to find it."

"Yeah, sure. I'll be right up," his voice assured him. "You take care, Marty. Good luck."

"Thanks, Lucas."

The door at the bottom of the fire stairs had the words "EMERGENCY EXIT ONLY" printed in fading but still bold black letters on it. "I think this is an emergency," he said softly as he pushed the door open and stepped out into a narrow alley.

Washington, DC

SPECIAL AGENT David Christopher shook his head slowly from side to side, "So what exactly are you telling me Norman?"

Computer Technician Norman Zight flexed his eyebrows several times before responding. "Well sir, in as much as we had a hit at JFK about ten minutes ago, and another at almost the same time at Chicago's O'Hare…." His voice trailed off.

"You telling me the damned system ain't worth shit, Norman?"

"Oh no sir!" Technician Zight bridled. "Not at all! The system is truly wonderful. It's just that not every camera's angle is as good as we would like it to be…" Norman managed a weak smile and a slight chuckle as he held up a still photo of John Gunner, "You know they say everybody has a double somewhere and this guy isn't exactly somebody who stands out in a crowd. "

"In other words the system is not reliable Norman. We really don't know if Gunner was in Atlantic City or Philadelphia or New York or Chicago or any other goddamn place."

"I'm certain the Atlantic City make was a good one. The camera was at eye level. His cap didn't hide anything and the glasses, well glasses don't do much to distort the image."

"Okay, Norman." Christopher leaned back in his chair. "I don't mean to give you a hard time. I know you guys do great work and nothing's one hundred percent accurate. I'll call Agent Shuman and tell her to come home. We could have been spinning a lot more wheels if you hadn't brought this to me right away quick. Thank you. I really appreciate it."

"Yes sir, you're welcome." Norman started to go then turned back, "We'll keep checking and let you know if we get any more hits."

"Thanks, Norman," David Christopher called after the disappearing technician then looked back at the coroner's report on his desk before picking up his telephone. He punched in Jane Shuman's number and waited for her to answer.

"Agent Shuman." Her voice sounded in his ear.

"How's it going Jane? Any luck?"

"No." The tone of her voice fully expressed her frustration. "We have been checking hotels near the bus station but so far no luck."

"Yeah, well I think you're probably on a wild goose chase…"

She waited a moment for him to say more before asking, "How come? What's up? What happened?"

"Norman just came to see me," he answered. "They found a couple more matches for our guy, one in New York and one in Chicago."

"Ohhh." Janet's groan said more than words.

"Yeah." Christopher agreed. "And just for icing on the cake, I have the autopsy report on Senator Anderson. He died from perfectly natural causes, a major coronary event."

"I'll be damned." Agent Shuman's voice sounded as deflated as he knew she was feeling. "So what do you make of this Gunner person?"

“I don’t make anything of him, Jane. Maybe he’s off on an assignment, maybe he’s on vacation, maybe he’s off his rocker, maybe he... Hell, who knows. Come on home, tomorrow we‘ll see if we can get anything more from Harry Gustafson.”

“On my way,” she told him.

Pittsburgh, PA.

IT HAD BEEN a long day for John Gunner when, just a few minutes past eight o'clock in the evening, Pete Sosnowski wheeled into the Best Western parking lot. There were enough trucks in the half full lot to make the sign "Truckers Welcome" superfluous. "If George is on the desk," Pete told him as he pulled on the hand break, "Tell him you came in with me. He'll give you a good rate."

"I don't know how to thank you, Pete." Gunner reached over to shake his hand.

"Forget it. I appreciate having someone to talk to. Now beat it, I got-a get this load in on time."

"I'm gone," Gunner grinned as he swung the door open. Climbing down from the cab he pulled his gym bag out from behind the seat, told the driver, "It was a great ride, Pete, thanks again," then slammed the door and headed for the motel lobby. He looked back and gave a last wave as Pete he released the breaks, eased the huge eighteen wheeler back onto the highway, and disappeared into the growing darkness. He owed Pete Sosnowski a lot. He owed Waitress Mary a lot more. It was her who hooked him up with Sosnowski. He congratulated himself again for having had the smarts to look for a ride out of Philly with a trucker; even more for asking Mary for help. He felt badly at having given her only a two dollar tip, he could have given her a lot more but he did not want her, or anyone, to think he was "flush." His story had been needing to get out of town because he owed people money that he didn't have. He had lost his job, used his credit card to the max, and now had nothing left. It was a story that was all too common these days.

There were security cameras in the lobby, but not ones to worry about. They were up high, with wide angle lenses. The long bill on the "Truckers of America" cap Pete had given him was probably all he really needed but he was careful to use his handkerchief and keep his head down.

George was not on the desk. "No, George is off tonight," the clerk told him. "I'm Oscar, can I help ya?"

"Yeah, I hope so. Pete Sosnowski just dropped me off, told me to say hello to George. He said maybe George could give me a rate is all. I just need a room for tonight, if ya got one."

"Yeah, sure. I know ol' Pete. I think maybe George is like his cousin er somethin, but I can fix ya up. Just one night?"

"I think so," Gunner answered. "I got-a check in the morning'. I might need ta stay a couple."

"No problem," Oscar told him as he pushed a registration form to him. "Rate's ninety-five a night but a friend-a Pete's I can let ya have it for seventy."

"Appreciate it, Oscar," Gunner told him as he reached into his pocket and pulled out a small roll of bills..

"Ya got a credit card?" Oscar asked.

"No, I don't believe in those damn things. I know too many people who got screwed by those credit card companies."

"Yeah, I hear ya," Oscar agreed. "But if you ain't got a credit card I can't leave the phone on in your room or let you run up any charges."

“That’s okay. I don’t need the phone and anything I need I’ll pay in advance.”

“Good by me.” Oscar picked up the money, put it in the cash drawer, then handed Gunner a key card, “Number 622.”

“Thanks, Oscar.”

For twenty-one bucks a night more the Best Western room was no better than his room at The Palms, but he was in Pittsburgh, he had a place to stay, and he felt reasonably secure.

Needwood Lake, Rock Creek Park

SEVEN O'CLOCK in the morning is really a lovely time of day Stephen Hunter thought, specially here in the park. The sun was just high enough to cast bright golden beams of light down through the new leaves on the trees. A perfect place for a camera enthusiast like himself to take wonderful pictures. Out on the lake a gentle breeze was making slight ripples in the water, it was hard to believe such a bucolic setting could exist only a few miles from the White House. He knew Harry Gustafson would be along in less than five minutes, the man was an absolute fanatic about keeping to a schedule. Here, behind this large rock just a few feet off the trail, was the perfect place to wait. The rock itself was hardly visible through the spruce trees and vines and standing behind it he and his camera would be completely hidden from the colonel. He heard approaching footsteps. It could be anybody but somehow he knew it was the colonel. For just a moment he wondered again if this was right - if Colonel Gustafson could really be a threat to the organization he had helped to build - but only for a brief moment. He had received the order; the fee had been paid… The colonel came into view. He waited until he was just opposite.

Gustafson stumbled as he turned towards the camera with a look of total disbelief on his face. Three more steps and he fell to the ground.

Joggers were approaching from the north. From that direction they could see him before they would find Gustafson lying in the path. They would expect him to have seen the fallen man. "HELP! HELP!" Hunter ran towards Gustafson's body. "Man Down. Help!" he shouted again as he and the two joggers reached

Gustafson. One man quickly dropped to his knees and began to give resuscitation while the other called 911 then took several pictures of his companion and Hunter as they bent over Harold Gustafson's body.

Office of the Attorney General

THE IMPOPRTANCE of the nomination of Kempton Jennings to be Attorney General was somewhat overlooked in the excitement surrounding the election of Franklin Wadsworth and his running mate Helen Langdon, the first woman Vice President of the United States, however those really attuned to the importance of the office were truly impressed. Nearly seventy years old, slender, silver haired Kempton Jennings was a man with impeccable credentials. So much so that, in spite of his long standing friendship with the new president, he had virtually no political enemies. As a result his nomination was unanimously confirmed by congress almost immediately.

For President Wadsworth, Jennings was far more than just his attorney general; he was his friend, his advisor, and trusted all-knowing confident, a roll he filled to an even greater degree for Helen Langdon when she became America's first woman president following Wadsworth's unexpected death shortly after beginning his second term. One of Jennings' first acts after assuming office had been to nominate Wilson Merrill for Director of the Federal Bureau of Investigation. Like Jennings, Merrill was quickly confirmed. Not surprisingly Merrill was a loyal and devoted supporter of the attorney general who went to great pains to keep his mentor fully appraised of all FBI activity. This was something the attorney general encouraged by scheduling regular weekly breakfast get-togethers, like today's.

"Well, there you are," the attorney general stood to welcome his guest. "I was about to start without you."

“Sorry Kempton. I’ve been on the phone. Some rather disturbing news I’m afraid…”

“Oh? Well sit down,” Jennings gestured to the chair opposite him, “Have some orange juice and tell me what’s up.”

“Yes. Thanks.” FBI Director Merrill did exactly as Kempton Jennings suggested, then, “Harry Gustafson dropped dead about an hour ago.”

“Jesus Christ!” The attorney general’s surprise and shock was obvious.

‘He was taking his regular morning run up in Rock Creek Park,” Merrill continued, “When he stumbled and fell. By the time anyone could get to him he was dead.”

“His heart?”

“Nothing official yet, but it certainly sounds like it. Just like Senator Anderson.” Merrill took a sip of coffee before adding, “You know the cameraman John Gunner worked for Gustafson.”

“Yes I do,” Jennings nodded, “And do we have any idea where Mr. Gunner is?”

“No, not yet. We’ve had a couple of leads, pretty certain he was in Atlantic City two days ago, then we think he turned up in Philadelphia.” Merrill smiled, “Just a matter of time before we find him Kempton. You know our people.”

“Yes, yes, the best in the world Wilson, I know they will catch up with the man, then perhaps we can find out what he’s all about.”

Pittsburgh, PA

GUNNER looked at his watch - "My god," he spoke out loud. It was almost ten o'clock. He had been awake most of the night. Awake - worrying - thinking - what to do next? Obviously he finally fell asleep and now he had to step on it, unless he was very mistaken check out time was eleven. The sleepless night had been nonproductive - he still had no particular idea where he would go today, or what he would do today, but a shower would give him a chance to wake up and think about such things.

He stood in the shower for almost ten minutes then got out, dried off, switched on the 10:30 TV News and began to dress. He ignored the commercial message, something to do with Erectile Dysfunction, paid little attention to the weather man's final pronouncement regarding the prospect for showers later this afternoon and only half heard the newscaster as he began his final report:

> *"Finally, from Washington, DC a sad story for all of us in the news business - Harold Gustafson, one of our own, collapsed and died this morning during his regular morning jog..."*

The shirt Gunner was putting on slipped from his fingers as he stared at the TV, neither hearing nor seeing anything further. Tears filled his eyes. The colonel... the man who had saved him, recruited him, given him the opportunity for revenge.... *"Don't think of this as revenge,"* the colonel had insisted. *"Revenge is not good. What you will be doing is helping to defend your country against an evil enemy."* Yes, he told himself, the evil enemy that killed my father, and my brother, and my mother. But now an even more evil enemy has taken the life of my commander, my friend… my second father.

Anger overcame him. Who issued the ordered? It had to come from Group 1. But why? No one was more loyal, more dedicated to G1 than Colonel Gustafson. Who is Group 1? Who runs it? The FBI? The CIA? The Army? The Defense Department? Who gives the orders? He had to find out. Find out and avenge the colonel's death. The colonel had breakfast with someone yesterday morning, someone who could resolve the problem. Did that person give the order? If not, does that person know who did? In spite of the questions tumbling about in his mind he knew what he had to do. Almost two years ago the colonel had given him an order: *"If anything should ever happen to me, go to my home as quickly as possible and clear out everything in my safe having to do with G One."* The colonel had given him a key to his condominium and insisted he memorize the safe's combination. It was etched in his mind, 4-8-7-1-4. Alright, no more running and hiding. Time for action. First, the colonel's safe, then find out who gave the order. Then eliminate him, or her, or them. That is his new assignment.

With trucker's cap and sun glasses carefully in place and head slightly bowed, Gunner walked to the front desk to turn in his room key.

"Everything okay?" the desk clerk asked.

"Just fine, thanks. I'm gonna get a little breakfast then I'm out of here.'

"Have a good day," the clerk told his receding back.

"What'll ya have?" the girl behind the counter asked as he sat down.

"Coffee and a donut's all I got time for, my ride's waitin'," he told her.

"See your bag's all packed and you're ready to roll. Where you headed," she asked as she poured coffee into an empty cup waiting on the counter.

"…Ah," he took a sip, hoping she would think he was being evasive. "Ah, west," he said at last. "Way west."

"Chicago, huh? Chicago or Cleveland's about the only place anybody goes from here… What kind-a donut? Cinnamon? Glazed?"

"Gimme a glazed," he answered. Then, as she started to reach for it, he changed his mind and told her he would have cinnamon. He hoped he had kept her attention long enough for her to remember him if anyone asked, remember he was headed west, to Cleveland, or maybe Chicago.

As he sipped his coffee and ate the cinnamon donut, in what he hoped would appear to be a thoughtless moment, he looked at his wrist watch, then glanced up at the clock on the wall as if to check the time; the clock just next to the security camera he spotted last night when he had eaten his late evening dinner. After a second or two he blinked and quickly lowered his head again. If the security computers were working as well as they were supposed to the brief look he had just given the camera should have been plenty to ID him.

Now minutes were counting. Under the best of circumstances he was sure it would take at least two minutes for the FBI Field Office in Pittsburgh to be alerted. Even if there was a police car standing in the hotel parking lot, it would take a couple of minutes more to down load a photo. He could not imagine an officer or an agent actually getting here in less than ten minutes, but he would allow himself only five. When they did come he wanted them to find the waitress he had just been talking to. Wanted her to tell them he was headed for Chicago. He finished the coffee, left half the donut, then made a point of leaving a big tip as he told the counter girl "thanks," before hurrying towards the exit door. He half thought about whistling "Chicago" on the way out but decided that might be overdoing it.

Several trucks in the parking lot had their engines running, two others were making their way towards the exit. Dodging between big rigs until he was well out of the restaurant's line of site he walked to the highway and to the bus stop he and Pete Sosnowski had spotted when they arrived last night. There he joined a group of several men and two women waiting for the next bus.

Together they waited… And waited…

One of the two women looked at her wrist watch, "Wouldn't you know," she said to her friend. "This morning the bus is late."

Damn!

A Pittsburgh police car moving at a fairly high speed came by, braked quickly, and turned into the motel parking lot.

Double damn! Maybe he should start to walk. No, that would just call attention to him. He looked back towards the parking lot - no sign of police; but from where he was he standing he could not see the hotel entrance.

"Well about time," the woman who had looked at her watch exclaimed.

Gunner looked down the road; a bus was coming towards them; slowing down; stopping. One elderly man got off. He was next to last to board.

Washington, D.C.

THIS MORNING'S MESSAGE to Aunt Sarah was a somewhat detailed description of the new dress she had just bought. Contained in the description was the information:

Subject still missing. Possible connection Gustafson death.

Beryl checked the message carefully then leaned back in her chair, took a sip of the coffee that had grown cold, and clicked "SEND."

On the other side of town NSA Annalist Martin Small took note of the blinking "alert" light signaling a new Beryl Kinney message.. Had it not been for the recent "Immediate Action" order regarding the woman he would not have placed an alert on her correspondence but under the circumstances he had felt compelled to do so. Sounds like a very expensive dress, he thought as he read the message a second time. It occurred to him that Beryl Kinney and Aunt Sarah had exchanged several messages in the last week or so, could this have some significance? A little more checking revealed the fact that Aunt Sarah's address was actually a "drop" from which messages were forwarded to unknown places. Perhaps he should send an addendum to the report he delivered the other day.

In her office three floors above Annalist Small's cubical, Section Chief Anna Watanobe read his addendum, then sent a request to DeCode asking for an analysis of the Beryl Kinney messages. A moment later, acting on something of a second thought, Section Chief Watanobe sent both of Annalist Small's reports to Victoria Phillips, her opposite member over at CIA with a note asking:

"Any knowledge of this Spanish connection?"

Twenty minutes after that a vibration under Beryl Kinney's left arm was so gentle, and so unexpected, that for a moment she did not realize what it was, but only for a moment. Then, with a casual head twist and back stretch, she turned away from her computer, got to her feet and headed for "The Ladies." There, inside booth 3, she unbuttoned the top of her blouse, reached under her left arm and retrieved her i-Phix. It took her less than two minutes to decode the message:

Sarah blown.
Discontinue use immediately.
Will advise new contact.

Pittsburgh, PA

THE CITY BUS dropped Gunner off two blocks beyond "Honest Al's." The faded pennants he had seen fluttering from the electric wire running from pole to pole together with the large hand painted price signs on the windshields of the cars lined up there told him all he needed to know: Honest Al dealt in low end used cars and, by the look of them, they were all well used.

As he walked slowly past the front line of cars a man came out of the small shack that apparently served as an office. "Good morning," he called as he approached and kicked away an empty coffee container that was lying on the ground. "Ya in the market fer a car?"

"Yeah, maybe," Gunner answered. "Depends."

"Everything depends," the man agreed. "Depends on the price and what-cha need. Depends on if ya can really appreciate the kind-a deal we can make fer ya here at Honest Al's." The man fell in step with Gunner. "Man like you probably wants something' fast and sexy like this little convertible here." He pointed to a red, two-seater Toyota with a $3,999 price tag on the windshield.

"Nothin' like that," Gunner told him. "I need something' dependable that don't cost an arm and a leg."

"Got just what-cha need right back in the second row." The salesman pointed towards a faded, silver, Subaru Forester with a $699 price tag on the window. "That baby gets great mileage and will take ya anywhere ya wanna go."

Gunner walked to the little SUV, opened the driver's side door and looked in. He didn't know a lot about automobiles but he thought the look of the upholstery could sometimes tell you as much as the odometer. The upholstery was well worn.

"What year?"

"This here's a two thousand nine, but don't let that fool ya, maybe a little old but she's been took care of. Got less than two hundred thousand miles on her and if you know anything about these here Subaru babies ya know they don't get broke in 'till they got that much on 'em."

"She got that location finder shit on her?" Gunner asked. LoJac had been a great idea once upon a time, and probably resulted in police finding a lot of stolen automobiles, but now, under Langhorn/Davis, every new car sold in the U.S. was required to be equipped with a location finder device so that Security Central could locate you any time they wanted to, at least locate your car anyway.

"Naw - this one's too early for that."

"Okay, good. Can I take her for a spin?"

"Sure. I'll get the keys and go with ya."

The motor sounded all right. The breaks seemed to work well and the car's steering was tight. At 55 there seemed to be no noticeable shimmy or shake.

"I'll give you five hundred for her," Gunner told the salesman when he pulled back into the car lot.

"You got-a be kiddin'," the salesman managed a half laugh. "I might let you have it for six-fifty, but five hundred. No way."

"Cash." Gunner said softly as he took bills out of his pocket. He spread them out so the man could see. There were exactly five one hundred dollar bills. "Either this, or I got-a look someplace else."

"Jesus, mister. You drive a hard bargain. Lemme check the books in the office."

"I got time," Gunner answered.

Less than three minutes later the salesman returned. "Look, you seem like a nice guy and you're my first customer today, so I wanna make a deal wit-chu. I can let-chu have the car for six hundred. That's the best I can do."

Gunner folded the five hundred dollar bills and put them back in his pocket. "Sorry, that's all I got," he told the man as he climbed out of the car. He pulled his gym bag out of the back seat and started to walk away. He almost reached the sidewalk before the man called after him:

"Shit! All right. You can have her for five."

Washington, DC

THE UNDER ARM VIBRATION was becoming a familiar interruption to Beryl Kinney's work day. This time, however, it came as she was in conversation with her section chief.

"You alright?" Her chief asked.

"Yeah," Beryl managed a slight laugh, "Just a twitch under my arm. Must have strained a muscle or something."

Several minutes later, section chief conversation completed, Beryl Kinney went to her usual booth in the women's rest room. The Eschelon message displayed on her I-Phix screen was not in code:

Albert Helms
Valencia Ave., Staten Island
Purchase 2009 Subaru Forester.
Pittsburgh, PA.

Pennsylvania Route 15

DRIVING SOUTH EAST Gunner was nearing Frederick, Pennsylvania, when the warm sun shining in his eyes and last night's sleeplessness began to catch up with him. The roadway shoulder was wide and numerous tire tracks made it obvious the shoulder was frequently used for parking. A coppice of trees producing a shadowed area a hundred or so yards up ahead looked like a perfect place for a nap, and a nap was exactly what he needed. Yes, he needed to get to DC, needed to take care of the colonel's business, but falling asleep at the wheel and running off the road was not something he wanted to do. Falling asleep while driving would very likely put an end to everything.

As he pulled off the road and into the shade he wondered why he had remembered a group of trees is called a "coppice." It was a word his father had used. Jesus, what strange things you remember. He could remember coppice, but he was damned if he had any idea what kind of trees he was parking in the shade of. No matter, a little sleep was what he needed, not tree names. He yawned, loosened his seat belt, tilted the seat back and yawned again.

A loud rapping noise awakened him. For a second or two he had no idea where he was or what was making the noise. He blinked his eyes… The rapping came again, it was at the window. He turned his head to look. Oh God, it was a policeman. How could they have found him? What could he do? Blinking sleep from his eyes he pressed the window button. Nothing. Hell, the engine wasn't running. He grabbed the door handle and opened the door. "Yes officer?"

The policeman grinned down at him. "You okay?"

"Okay?" The question surprised him. "Ahhh, yeah. Wha, what-a you mean?"

"I mean," the officer laughed, "I mean I thought you might be dead. You were really cuttin' wood."

"Oh," he was waking up, "Yes, I bet I was. I didn't realize how tired I was…am."

"Well you did the right thing pulling in here for a nap. People driving sleepy cause all sorts of problems. Sorry I woke you up."

"Oh, please don't apologize, it's good to know you guys are out here watching over us."

"Well we try." The officer straightened up. "Sleep some more, I won't bother you again."

"Thanks officer," Gunner called after him.

It was past noon when he awoke for the second time. Not to a policeman knocking on his window this time, but to the sounds of a Pennsylvania National Guard convoy making its slow way up the highway. "I'm glad they aren't looking for me," Gunner told himself as the last of the dozen or so trucks slowly passed, but there were people who are, he remembered, and it was time to be moving.

Washington, DC

GUNNER KNEW D.C. POLICE are notorious for picking on out of town cars for even the most miniscule violations so he was extra careful as he drove along 16th Street next to Rock Creek Park. He had used his Albert Helms ID to register the car but if he were stopped by the police it would take no time at all for them to uncover his true identity and it would all be over. It was not yet four o'clock when he parked around the corner from Colonel Gustafson's home just off Kaimia Road. He had circled the block twice before parking and spotted nothing indicating the place was under surveillance, so, okay, let's do it. Before getting out of the Subaru he pulled on a pair of the plastic gloves he bought at a drug store several miles back. No finger prints would be left in the colonel's house. With his still camera over his shoulder and his gloved hands shoved into his jacket pockets, he walked casually to the front gate.

4-8-7-1-4. Click. The safe opened. It was virtually empty. Empty except for his video camera and a small plastic case in which four digital cards resided; cards John Gunner knew very well, four batteries, eight lethal charges. Nothing else in the safe but the batteries and the camera were quite enough; he could not guess what questions would have arisen had they been discovered by someone outside G1. Should he look any further? No, the colonel had instructed him to clean out the safe, that was all he was to do. It was time to go. Time to find "them." Closing the safe, he spun the combination dial then slipped the plastic battery case into his jacket pocket, picked up the video camera and started towards the door.

"Jesus Christ!" He was amazed at how loud his voice sounded but he was even more amazed at what he was looking at. How in the name of God could he have overlooked it when he came in? Apparently he had been so intent on the safe that he never even looked at the other side of the room, at the colonel's desk, at the video camera resting there. A camera just like his video camera. A camera complete with the TVNews logo and his initials on it. Obviously the colonel had intended to substitute this camera for his. This camera with no electronic bullet capability, no hint of G1. Well, if the that is what the colonel intended it ought to have some of his fingerprints on it… Carefully removing the plastic gloves and making certain not to touch anything else, Gunner picked up the substitute camera, switched it on and off several times then clicked "playback." He was surprised to find coverage of Senator Anderson's remarks; he had not realized he had taken the pictures.

Okay, all ready for whoever might find it; plenty of prints and the digital card he recorded on still in his camera. He put it back on the desk and pulled the plastic gloves back on. Time to go. Time for his own assignment.

29th Street - Georgetown

HAPPILY, he could see the “Room for Rent” sign still in Mrs. Aims window as he walked towards her front door. Before heading to her house he had located a small self-storage warehouse where he convinced the attendant he was involved in a messy divorce and needed to put some things in a locker his about to be ex-wife couldn’t find. He paid for six months in advance and a fifty dollar tip persuaded the man let him use a fake name and address. The video camera and the disks would be safe there until he was ready to use them.

Wha-chu doin’ back here?” Mrs. Aims wanted to know. “Thought you was goin’ ta work in Arlington.”

“Thought so too,” Gunner answered. “Didn’t work out the way though, so I need a room again for a few days.”

“Same room’s available; same price,”

Okay.” He handed her three hundred dollars. “I’m glad to have it.”

The room was like an old friend. He pushed his bag under the bed then went into the tiny bathroom to wash his hands. Next on his “to-do” list was find an AT&T store. Tomorrow was going to be a busy day and he needed a phone to make some very important calls with. Calls from a phone he could quickly dispose of.

Rock Creek Park

JOHN GUNNER WALKED a few hundred feet away from the bus stop. He looked again at the early morning sun reflecting off the lake and listened again to the gentle lapping of the waves against the shore, the whispering breeze, the chirping birds. He wasn't sure why he had decided to make his first call from the park, maybe because this is where the colonel died, maybe because this was where he saw the colonel for the last time, maybe just because it was easy to get there by bus. He didn't want to use his "new car" any more than necessary, it was safely parked on a side street where there was no parking restriction other than Monday mornings between 8AM and 11AM. Alright, he told himself, never mind the birds and the breeze I have a job to do. He punched the number for the news desk into the keyboard of his brand new "GoPhone." AT&T had required no ID when, using the name Donald Bowen, he paid cash for the phone and $10 worth of pre-paid calling.

After three beeps a familiar voice answered, "News Desk, Kline."

"George, it's John Gunner…."

"John!" George Kline's tone of voice expressed his surprise. "Where the hell are you? People been looking all over for you."

"Never mind where I am, what happened to Harry?"

"Oh God." George's voice instantly changed from surprise to sadness. "You can't believe it, John. Tuesday he came back from a breakfast meeting over at the Woodland, went into his office and pretty much kept to himself all day. Maybe he wasn't feelin' too good but he never said anything, then yesterday morning he dropped dead over in Rock Creek Park."

"I'll be damned." Gunner paused for a moment as his brain started to focus on what George Kline had just told him. "George, I'll get back there as soon as I can." He switched off the GoPhone without listening to whatever else Kline had to say.

It stood to reason the "people" George said were looking for him included the FBI and George would even now be on the telephone telling them he had just heard from him and giving them the number he had called form. It would take about thirty seconds to put a trace on future calls from that phone; another couple of minutes to learn when and where he bought it... Okay, he told himself, now they know I'm in DC and it will be a easy for them to locate the place where any future calls from this phone come from. They might even be able to learn where I made this call to the news desk from. It's time to ditch the phone, time to leave the park. There were several benches at the bus stop, he left the phone on one of them. Just maybe someone will pick it up and use it, he thought. That could create a little confusion.

The Woodland Park Hotel was well known to John Gunner. It was an elegant apartment hotel where he had taped any number of interviews with various Washington big wigs who maintained residences there. He knew the service entrance, the service elevators, and all the back ways to nearly everywhere in the building. Not only did he know the hotel well, he knew Richard Zwerline. "Rich" was the assistant manager who handled security. He was always in charge of getting TV crews into and out of the building without disturbing guests. Rich would know who the colonel had breakfast with.

The call to Richard Zwerline from a second GoPhone was everything he hoped for. Rich felt terrible about the colonel's death. Tuesday morning Rich had seen him in the restaurant having breakfast with C. Gordon Wolfe. It took Gunner a second or two to realize what Zwerline had just told him. "C. Gordon Wolfe?" He asked. "The vice president's chief of staff C. Gordon Wolfe?"

"Yeah, none other," Zwerline answered. "Harry and I said a couple of words to each other. He looked fine to me. I can't believe he dropped dead the next day."

FBI Headquarters

THE DOOR to Special Agent David Christopher's office was closed but it was okay because in addition to Jane Shuman, Special Agent Mark Winter and Computer Tech Norman Zight were on hand. As Jane looked around the thought came to her mind, "I guess they don't worry about gang rape." The resulting grin on her face caught Special Agent Christopher's attention.

"If there is something funny going on here, Special Agent Shuman, I do wish you would share it with the rest of us. Right now I could use a laugh or two."

"Sorry, sir," she could not hide an even larger grin. "Must have been something I ate."

"Yes." Christopher raised his eyebrows, "Of course, bagels for lunch. Never a good idea." He nodded his head up and down before continuing. "All right, let's be sure we're all on the same page. Here's the situation: On May 21st Charles Young, in Senator Orin Anderson's office, received a phone call from a TVNews cameraman named John Gunner warning him the senator was in danger and asking Mr. Young to meet him so he could give him details. Mr. Young agreed to meet Gunner at a restaurant, then called us. Jane, you and Mark went to intercept Mr. Gunner but he never showed. Right?"

"Right," Jane agreed.

"The following morning," Chris continued, "Senator Anderson died as the result of very unexpected heart attack. Yesterday morning Mr. Gunner's boss, TVNews Director Harold Gustafson, died as the result of what was apparently a similar, sudden, unexpected heart attack. We have no knowledge of any contact Mr. Gustafson and Mr. Gunner may have had prior to that, but we would like to talk to Mr. Gunner and we can't find him." Agent Christopher glanced up from his notes, "Is that about where we stand?"

"Yes," Agent Shuman answered as Mark Winter and Norman Zight nodded agreement. "I think it is also important to remember that last month Mr. Gunner was one of the reporters covering Sheik al-Sameur's arrival," she added. "The Sheik had come to Washington to meet with Senator Anderson's committee. He also died suddenly, unexpectedly, from a heart attack."

"Yes he did." Chris nodded his head in agreement. "That's three heart attacks, three dead men, each man in one way or another connected to John Gunner." Agent Christopher glanced quickly at each of his listeners, "Any thoughts?"

"Are you suggesting John Gunner is somehow causing these heart attacks, Chris?" Agent Winter asked.

"No, not yet Mark, Not yet." Chris answered, then continued, "At eight o'clock yesterday morning John Gunner apparently had breakfast in Pittsburgh and told the waitress he was going to Chicago, then…"

"We're certain on that one Chris," Computer Tech Norman Zight interjected. "He definitely was in Pittsburgh yesterday morning."

"Good enough, Norm," Christopher responded. "And if he was, he was not here in Washington when Harry Gustafson died. But this morning he turned up here in DC and made a call to TVNews from a phone he purchased at an AT&T store over on Madison. Thanks to… what's his name? The news desk man over at TVNews..."

“George Kline,” Jane Shuman said softly.

“Yeah, George Kline,” Christopher paused to check his notes again, “Thanks to Mr. Kline we know Gunner apparently had just learned of Harold Gustafson’s death. Kline said he was very upset and wanted to know how it happened. He said he told Gunner how Mr. Gustafson collapsed while on his regular morning jog in Rock Creek Park.“ Chris glanced at Jane Shuman, “You talked with him Jane, is that about what he said?”

“A couple-a-things more,” Jane answered. “Mr. Kline also said he told Mr. Gunner Harry Gustafson had not seemed himself after coming back from a breakfast meeting over at the Woodland Park Hotel Tuesday morning.”

“Yes, right,” Chris nodded agreement. “We should probably check out who he was meeting with…”

“C. Gordon Wolfe,” Jane broke in.

“C. Gordon Wolfe?” The surprise in Chris’ voice was unmistakable.

“Yes, and John Gunner knows that too.”

Chris’ eyes widened and his nostrils flared slightly as his vocal expression of surprise now became visual as well. “He does? How do you know all this?”

“I talked with a Mr. Zwerline who is in charge of security at the Woodland. He saw Gustafson and Wolfe having breakfast together. He told me Mr. Gunner telephoned him this morning - must have been just after he talked with George Kline - Zwerline knows Mr. Gunner from news assignments he has been involved with at the hotel. Mr. Gunner asked Mr. Zwerline if he knew what had happened to Gustafson. Mr. Zwerline remembers telling him how shocked he was at the news and how he seemed fine when he having breakfast with C. Gordon Wolfe,” Jane paused, then added, “He remembers Mr. Gunner saying something about needing to call Mr. Wolfe.”

“Ouch!” Christopher’s eyes widened. “This is getting dicey. Just what the hell is going on here?”

Agent Shuman was the first to answer: “I don‘t think we have an answer to that Chris, but remembering Mr. Gunner called Senator Anderson‘s office to warn him,” she hesitated a moment, then suggested, “Maybe he wants to warn Mr. Wolfe too?” She put it as a question.

“Jesus, you could be right Jane. We have got to find John Gunner quickly.”

“He is top priority at Computer Central,” Norman Zight proclaimed.

“Good Norman.” Chris gave him a thumbs up. “Any suggestions as to what more we can do?”

“I have one or two,” Jane said after a moment’s silence.

“And they are?…” Chris asked.

“Well, for one thing I think we should alert Mr. Wolfe,” Jane continued. “Mr. Gunner’s calls sometimes have unexpected results.”

“Jesus yes! I‘ll call his office right away. Better yet, I‘ll ask the director to call him.”

“Also,” Jane said slowly, “Mr. Kline indicated Mr. Gunner’s call came as something of a surprise because they hadn’t heard from him for a several days but during that time they had received two phone calls from a woman named Beryl Kinney asking for information about his whereabouts. I’m curious as to who Ms. Kinney is. I think we should try to learn something about her.”

Chris nodded agreement, "Good idea, Jane."

"And finally," Jane added after what could only be termed a pregnant pause, "I've been thinking, since we aren't having much success finding John Gunner by ourselves why don't we put him on TV?"

"Now that's a hell of an idea, Jane. Three great ideas actually." Agent Christopher's sincerity was obvious as he added, "You get after the TV people, I'll talk to the director right away and let's all of us see what we can find out about Beryl Kinney."

As Chris began to gather up his notes Special Agent Mark Winter looked up from the papers he had been shuffling through. "I know who Beryl Kinney is," he announced.

What?" From Agent Christopher

"Who?" From Agent Shuman.

"You do?" From Computer Technician Norman Zight.

"Yeah… I thought the name sounded familiar; she lives in the apartment across the hall from John Gunner. I noted the names on all the mail boxes when I went to interview the landlord. I asked him about each of the tenants. Ludenthall, he's the landlord, said she moved in March 15th."

"Great work, Mark." Chris grinned and tipped an imaginary hat towards him. "See what else you can find out about her."

Mrs. Aims' Rooming House

JOHN GUNNER stretched out on his bed and closed his eyes. He wasn't sleepy, he wasn't even tired. Quite the contrary, he was revved up and needed to be quite for a few minutes and review what he had learned today. First, the newspaper report on the colonel's death: "*An amateur photographer and two joggers found the body.*" The "amateur photographer" had to be a G1 Agent. Second, the information that the colonel had breakfast with C. Gordon Wolfe. That would seem to mean Wolfe is the man who could have re-instated him. Could C. Gordon Wolfe be the person who runs G1? Wolfe is the vice president's Chief of Staff, but is that far enough up the ladder to command Group 1? More likely it is his boss - the vice president. That makes more sense. But how to be sure… he needed some proof. How to get proof? Well, the phone call he made to Wolfe's office an hour ago might stir things up, might bring some information to light:

"You have reached the office of C. Gordon Wolfe," a disembodied coldly official female voice advised him after the third ring. *"If you have reached this number by mistake, please hang-up. If you wish to leave a message press one, wait for the tone, then leave your message. If a reply is required, this office will contact you.*" He pressed 1, waited for the tone and left the message: *"This is John Gunner. I have been ordered to photograph Mr. Wolfe. Please tell him I can do that at his convenience in the next day or two."*

If C. Gordon Wolfe or the vice president run G1 that message certainly ought to get some attention, Gunner told himself. But now what? How would he learn if there was any reaction to his call? He swung his feet off the bed and stood up. The room had become too small, too claustrophobic. He needed some fresh air. He needed to take a walk.

The day had been warm and the breeze now rustling leaves on the trees along 29th Street was most welcome. He walked slowly enjoying deep breaths of the fresh, cool air. What do I do next, he asked himself. Maybe "let the pot boil," as his mother used to say. Let C. Gordon Wolfe get his message and think about it. Maybe the next move should be Wolfe's. It may have been the thought of his mother's boiling pot that made him realize how hungry he was. He looked at his wristwatch, nearly seven o'clock. No wonder he was hungry, he had not eaten anything all day. He knew there was a Rib-Joint only a few blocks away from Mrs. Aims' house, he had smelled the aroma of barbecuing ribs other times when he walked in the area. Barbecued Ribs sounded like a very good idea.

In the sitting room at the back of her house, with a small amount of Early Times Kentucky Whisky, a like amount of tap water and two ice cubes in her glass, Mrs. Aims settled into her rocking chair to watch the seven o'clock news. Mrs. Aims seldom missed the evening news, or her Kentucky Bourbon. Both the whiskey and the news program were finishing when the news anchor told her audience:

> *"One last note in our news today, The FBI is anxious to talk with a man named John Gunner. Here is a picture of Mr. Gunner,"*

The image on the TV screen changed from the news woman to two still pictures of Gunner: one with a beard, one without.

> *"It is believed Mr. Gunner is somewhere here in the DC area."*

Her voice continued over Gunner's pictures.

If you happen to know him, or if you have
recently seen him, please telephone the
Federal Bureau of Investigation at the number
on your screen."

The screen image switched back to the anchor woman.

"That's it for tonight,
I'm Caroline Smith, Thank you for watching.
I hope to see you all here again same time tomorrow.
Good night now."

Mrs. Aims knocked over her almost empty glass of Kentucky Whiskey as she reached for the telephone.

The three agents assigned to telephone duty were somewhat surprised by the number of calls they received almost immediately after Caroline Smith went off the air but, being skilled at their jobs, they were able to quickly separate the "nut calls" from those seeming to have information of value. It was the ninth call Agent Robinson took that rang the bell:

"This is Mrs. Aims. I live on North West 29th Street. I think that man you looking for is renting a room here in my house. Only he told me his name is Bowen."

"Thank you for calling Mrs. Aims. Can you tell me a little more about this man. When did he move into your house?"

"Well, he was here for a couple-a days about a week ago, then he come back yesterday. Said the job he went to in Arlington didn't work out and he needed the room again."

Agent Robinson pressed a button to alert David Christopher as he asked, "Is he in the room now Mrs. Aims?"

"No, I don't think so. I heard him go out 'bout an hour ago. I don't think he come back yet, least I ain't heard him. You want me ta go look?"

"No, I don't think that would be a good idea, Mrs. Aims." Robinson heard a click telling him Christopher had picked up. "Mrs. Aims, my supervisor would like to talk with you for a minute please."

"Yes, all right. I'm glad if I can help."

Apartment C - Cherry Avenue

MRS. AIMS' SURPRISE at the seven o'clock news story was duplicated in Beryl Kinney's apartment. She had just switched on her TV and poured herself a glass of Bogel Chardonnay when:

"Good God!" She exclaimed out loud.

The sight of John Gunner's name and picture on the screen caused such a strong reaction that, without realizing it, she snapped the delicate stem of her wine glass. What the hell is going on, she wondered. Realizing her glass was broken and she was bleeding, she headed to her bathroom to find a Band-Aid for the injured finger. Then her doorbell rang.

"Jesus," she muttered, "What now?"

She flipped the intercom switch, "Yess??"

"Miss Kinney?"

"Yes," she said again.

"Miss Kinney, I'm FBI Special Agent Anne Clark, I'm here with Special Agent Mark Winter, I wonder if we might have a word with you."

"FBI? How do I know you're FBI?" She asked. "And why do you want to talk to me?"

“We’ll be happy to show you our credentials.” the voice answered, “And the reason for our visit is to learn if you have any information that might help us locate Mr. John Gunner.”

29th Street NW

THE RIBS had been better than good. Together with a ton of fried potatoes and a schooner of beer, Gunner had eaten two large slabs of ribs and now felt almost too full to walk. When you're too full to walk the best thing you can do is walk, he told himself. A mile or so later he decided it was time to head for home.

There are street lights in Georgetown, there are also lots of trees and shrubs in Georgetown. This year's April showers, combined with unusually warm weather since then, had produced a bumper crop of leaves which did a good job of blocking the light from many of Georgetown's street lights. As a result, the sidewalks were mostly dark and, in the case of ageing cement, sometimes a bit treacherous. A fact John Gunner discovered just as he turned into 29th Street when an unexpected crack caught his toe and almost caused him to fall. "Pick up your feet, Edward," he could hear his mother's voice telling him. Jesus, he thought, I haven't been Edward in so many years. The unexpected thought of his mother quickly brought to mind the evening walks he use to take with her, his father, and his brother when he was a little boy. When he was Edward Spalding. The thought brought sudden tears to his eyes. He stopped, leaned against a tree and used his thumbs to wipe away the moisture.

Four days after the president had declared, "Mission Accomplished," in Iraq, his father, Colonel Philip Spalding, was killed by a road side bomb. Fifteen years later his brother, only two years out of West Point, was captured, tortured and beheaded in Iraq. And his mother… A reporter brought a picture of his decapitated brother to show her, to get her reaction. Her heart failed. Home on emergency leave from West Point, Edward

Spalding got a revolver that had belonged to his father and shot the bastard. While he was in jail Colonel Gustafson came to see him. That was when Edward Spalding died and he became John Gunner.

As he stood there, thinking of the family he once had, he became aware of an automobile stopping in front of Mrs. Aims' house. And aware of the fact that her front porch light was on. Not the usual situation, he thought, Mrs. Aims must be entertaining.

As he watched, two people got out of the automobile: a man and a woman. Oh Shit! It was the woman he had seen at The Place. She was half a block away, but there was something about her, about the way she carried herself that he found fascinating and memorable. He watched as the two walked to the doorway, rang the bell, then waited. A moment later the door opened and the man and the woman each held out something to, well he was sure it was to Mrs. Aims even though he could not see her. He knew damn well they were showing her their badges as they entered her house.

"Jesus," he whispered to himself. "If I hadn't tripped on that damn crack…." he didn't finish the thought as he turned away from the house and walked casually to the Subaru Forester parked a block away.

The Subaru started quickly. He switched on the headlights, pulled away from the curb and headed east to the Stop sign at 29th Street. The house was a block and a half away but the porch light was bright enough for him to see it. As far as he could tell there was no activity outside the house. He didn't think a car this far down the street would be cause for them to react, but then he hadn't thought there was any possible way for them to find his hideaway either.

"Damn!" He said out loud. "How the hell did they do that?"

Easy. Worry about it later, for now, pay attention to your driving. Okay, where do you wanna go? He asked himself as he made the right hand turn into 29th Street. He honestly didn't know. When he reached M Street he turned left and headed into the city.

Suddenly, unexpectedly, flashing lights a couple of blocks behind him… Oh Jesus! He made a quick right hand turn, switched off his lights. Waited… Watched in the rear view mirror… Okay, an ambulance, it was just an ambulance, not the cops. He turned around and went back to M Street.

M Street North-West eventually became M Street North-East and still he had no idea where he was going. He really needed to think and he couldn't do that and keep his mind on driving, what he needed was a place to park, and think. The bright lights of an all night gas station in the block ahead caught his eye. He should fill the tank no matter where he was going and the station might be a place to park for a while and concentrate on that. He pulled up to a "Service Only" pump. $9.89 a gallon! What the hell, the extra two dollars would eliminate the need for him to go into the store where the ever present security cameras would be watching.

"It's two bucks less if ya serve ya-self," a disheveled, grumpy looking older man told him as he opened his window.

"Yeah, I know, but I got-a bad leg. It's worth the extra money not to hurt."

"Yeah, Okay," the man said reluctantly. Obviously he had no interest in servicing customers. "Gimme ya card."

"Don't have one," Gunner told him as he handed a one hundred dollar bill out the window. "Don't trust them fuckers. You blow one payment and they got-cha fer life."

"I hear ya," the man took the bill. "Wan me ta fill er up?"

"Yeah, if it'll go that far," Gunner laughed.

“I hear ya,” the man said again.

The car took a little more than eight gallons, $90.13 worth to be exact. The service man hung up the hose and shuffled off as he called, “Back wid your change in a minute.” The “minute” turned into four or five minutes but he finally returned with Gunner’s change.

“Thanks,” Gunner told him as he pointed to the empty parking area on the far side of the station lot. “Listen, I’m kind-a pooped. Be okay if I pull over there and catch a quick nap?”

“Hell yeah. You can stay there all night if ya-wanna. And we got coffee inside if ya need it.”

Gunner parked, switched off the engine again, loosened his seat belt and tried to relax. Okay, just where the hell am I? He asked himself. Somehow his hide-out at Mrs. Aims house was blown. That was scary, very scary. What could he have done to give himself away? He could not think of making any mistakes that would reveal the rooming house but, regardless of that, it was blown. The question now is what’s my present situation and what should I do next? His gym bag and most of his clothing were back there in the room. Well, all that is gone but the good news is he never went anywhere without his money belt and his still camera, and fortunately it had been cool enough when he went out for something to eat that he had worn his jacket and, as was always the case, his cap - both being of the Redskins variety. Clothes and the bag he could replace. The real question was where the hell should he go now?

The rooming house idea had been a good one. At least he had thought so. Regardless, he was not going to find another one at this time of night. He checked his wrist watch, nearly 10 o‘clock. No, the only place to get a room at this time of night was a hotel or motel, or sleep in the car. Sleeping in the car did not appeal to him, but hotels and motels spelled security cameras and, with the luck he was having tonight, that didn't seem like a good idea. In fact it probably wasn't a good idea to stay anywhere near DC. Okay. He had a full tank of gas, so where should he go? Of course, Philadelphia. The Palms security camera was easy to duck and Lucas had been a friend. How long would it take him to drive to Philly? About a hundred fifty miles… shouldn't take more than three hours or so, maybe another hour to find his way to the hotel. He looked again at his watch, that would put him there sometime around one-thirty, two o'clock. But Lucas wouldn't be on duty at 2 o'clock in the morning. It would be the night man. What was his name? He couldn't remember it. Well, he would have several hours to think of it. Meanwhile maybe he could get a cup of coffee inside then be on his way.

Thinking to check out security camera locations, he walked to where he could see into the store through the large plate glass windows. The old man was watching TV… the ten o'clock news it looked like.

"Wholly shit!!!" Gunner said out loud. His picture had just appeared on the TV screen. Two pictures actually, one with his old beard, one without. And in large letters underneath his picture the words: "FBI - 800-555 3728." Mrs. Aims must have been watching TV! He no longer felt the need for a cup of coffee.

Mrs. Aims' House

"I'M BEGINNING TO THINK this is another adventure like The Place," Jane Shuman said as she looked at her watch for the tenth time in the last half-hour. "Don't ask me why, but he isn't going to show."

"I suspect you're right," Chris agreed. "We should go. Mark and Patrick can keep an eye on things from outside and we can let Mrs. Aims get some sleep."

"Oh it's alright, you needn't need-a go." Mrs. Aims stifled a yawn as she spoke. "I never had no FBI visitors before. It's kind-a excitin'."

"Well you have been very kind, Mrs. Aims, and very helpful," Jane told the woman. "We want you to know the FBI is grateful for your assistance, but it's time we let you get a little rest."

"Yes, indeed." Chris stood to leave. "There will be two agents in a car up the street incase Mr. Gunner, ah, Mr. Bowen, returns, but they won't bother you. Agent Shuman and I appreciate your hospitality. You have our cards, if you hear from Mr. Bowen, please give us a call."

"Yes. Yes, I will," Mrs. Aims assured them as she followed the two agents down the hall, past the room where John Gunner had been living, and to her front door. "Good night," she told them.

"Good night Mrs. Aims," Jane replied. "And thank you again."

Fifteen minutes later Agent Christopher pulled up in front of Agent Shuman's apartment building. "Hardly seems worth going to bed," Jane yawned as she looked at her wrist watch and started to slide out of the car. "It's two o'clock now and we have to meet with C. Gordon Wolfe at nine."

"And we don't want be late," both Jane and Chris echoed Director Merrill's instructions at the same time.

Philadelphia, PA.

BENNY. Gunner had remembered the night man's name, it was Benny. And finding the hotel had not been as difficult as he thought it might be. It was only a couple of minutes after two and all he had to do now was find a place to park. Easier said than done. He cruised around several blocks then remembered the alley behind the hotel. There had been a couple of cars parked there the morning he emergency exited.

Aside from the "No Parking - Fire Exit" sign alongside the hotel's emergency door he did not see any other restriction signs, so he parked behind a pick-up truck a hundred feet further up the alley, locked the car, and headed for the corner. Just for the hell of it he tried the emergency exit door. It was locked tight, as he expected it would be.

Trying to picture the hotel lobby as he climbed the stairs alongside the beauty shop, he remembered the fake palm tree and the old fashion check-in desk at the far end of the lobby. The security camera high above the desk didn't worry him greatly, it seemed to be focused more on the palm tree than on customers; with his head bowed and his cap pulled down he didn't think it would be much of a threat.

"You must be Benny," he said to the elderly man dozing in a chair behind the counter.

The man blinked his eyes then reached for a pair of glasses sitting on top of the old fashion file cabinet standing next to his chair. "Yeah, yeah. Who are you?"

"I'm Marty Fields. Lucas told me your name last time I was here."

"Oh yeah?" The man put on his glasses as he got out of his chair. "So what can I do for you? Lookin' fer a room?"

"Yes," Gunner answered.

"Sign in. Wha'd Lucas charge ya last time?"

"Forty-nine bucks."

"Okay. Pay in advance."

"I know that," Gunner grinned as he wrote "Ken Radcliff - Gary, Indiana" in the registration book then pulled a small roll of bills from his pocket. He peeled off four tens and two fives, handed them to the man and told him. "If three-fourteen is available, I'd like it."

.

Benny studied the key rack for several seconds before selecting a key. "Looks like the best I can do is three-twelve. It's right next door, just the other side-a the fire stairs."
"That'll do fine, thanks, Benny."

As Benny handed him the key he glanced down at the registration form Gunner had just filled out, "Ken Radcliff? Thought you was Marty Fields."

"Yeah, that was last time," Gunner laughed. "But you can tell Lucas Marty's back."

"Okay Marty. Goodnight."

Washington, DC

"YOU ARE FBI AGENTS Christopher and Simon?"

"Shuman," Jane told the woman at the same time as Chris said, "Good morning, yes we…."

The woman cut him off before he could finish his sentence, "I am Marion Harwood, Mr. Wolfe's assistant, may I see your identification."

With only a very quick glance at his partner, Agent Christopher produced his badge and ID photo. It took Jane a few seconds longer to retrieve hers from the shoulder bag she carried. The woman made a project of examining each photograph and comparing them to the two people facing her. Satisfied at last, she pointed to a doorway, "Please wait in the conference room, Mr. Wolfe will be with you shortly.

"Thank you Miss Harwood," Chris told the woman as he gestured for Jane to precede him.

The conference room was as coldly unfriendly as the woman assistant who had welcomed them but being acutely aware that any comments they might make would likely be recorded Jane and Chris silently took seats on opposite sides of the conference table. Words were not at all necessary anyway, the looks they exchanged said it all, "What a Bitch!"

"Your meeting with Mr. Wolfe is scheduled for 9 AM," Director Merrill had told them. "Don't be late. Mr. Wolfe does not like to be kept waiting." It was nearly 9:15 before Mr. Wolfe made his appearance.

Cornelius Gordon Wolfe, III was named after his father and grandfather but young Cornelius became unhappy with his first name when the nickname "Corny" befell him soon after he entered Exeter pre-school. As a result, when he reached prep-school, he decided to replace his first name with the initial C. "I'm C. Gordon Wolfe," he told his new companions. "Gordon to my friends." In addition to removing the "Corny" nickname, this name usage had the additional advantage of identifying him as separate and apart from his father who was well known in banking circles as "Cornelius Wolfe." Following in his father's footsteps C. Gordon attended Harvard, where he earned a law degree, then went to work at AllWorldOil as an administrative assistant to one of his father's fraternity brothers, Senior Vice President Donald Harris. C. Gordon quickly became known for his tireless energy, devoted attention to the wishes of his superiors, and complete comfort at bending the rules when it seemed desirable to do so. Five years later he had already become a junior vice president when AWO's chairman and president, Theodore Armstrong Dexter, left the corporate world for the world of politics and asked Gordon to become his Chief of Staff. Without even a second thought, the young man eagerly accepted the invitation and, in his mind at least, "Dex" Dexter could have found no one more perfect for the position.

"Don't get up," Wolfe signaled for them to remain seated as he joined them and carefully placed a slim file folder on the table before seating himself. "Do I understand you have some questions regarding a telephone call my office received from John Gunner?"

"Yes sir," Chris answered. "Actually you have answered our first question - you did receive a call from Mr. Gunner."

"That is correct." Wolfe's nostrils flared slightly in what Jane took to be annoyance. "Why is it of interest to you?"

“Shortly before his death Senator Anderson’s office received a warning call from Mr. Gunner…” Chris paused before adding, “We are anxious to know if his call to you was of a similar nature.”

“A warning?” Jane noticed Wolfe’s eyebrows twitch slightly as he answered. Something about the phone call he’s uncomfortable with she told herself. “No,” Wolfe continued, “It had to do with wanting to take my picture.”

“We’re anxious to contact Mr. Gunner.” Chris continued. “Did he leave a call back number?”

“I don’t know,” Wolfe shook his head slightly. “I didn’t actually listen to his message. Miss Harwood can give you a transcript if you like.”

“Thank you sir. The actual recording would be even better. Sometimes we can detect locations and sources…”

“Very well. I’ll have Marion get that for you.”

“Sir…” Agent Shuman began, “We understand TVNews.Gov comes under your purview, is that correct?”

Somewhat surprised by Jane’s question Wolfe blinked twice before replying. “That is basically correct... One of Vice President Dexter’s numerous concerns is supervision of that organization, a responsibility he has partially delegated to me…”

Jane did not think the man was aware of her slight facial reaction to his suddenly assumed pontifical tone of voice. She knew Chris was.

Managing to suppress the smile Jane’s look was threatening to cause, Chris picked up, “We understand Mr. Gunner reported to Harry Gustafson who met with you the day before his tragic death. Did Mr. Gustafson happen to make any mention of John Gunner during that meeting."

Wolfe looked in his file folder, took a pen from his pocket and made a brief notation before responding, "Mr. Gunner is a cameraman/reporter for TVNews.Gov, and he did indeed report to Harry Gustafson," he said slowly as he blinked what Jane believed were real tears from his eyes, "You know, this is very difficult. Harry was a close friend…"

After waiting a moment for Wolfe to say more, in her softest, most sympathetic voice, Jane told him, "Yes sir, we understand. We will try to get through with this as quickly as possible. Can you tell us if Mr. Gustafson said anything at all about John Gunner? Anything that might give us some idea where we could find him?"

"As a matter of fact, young lady," Wolfe took a handkerchief from his pocket and murmured, "Pardon me," as he lightly blew his nose… "As a matter of fact," he began again, "John Gunner was the subject of our meeting." Wolfe paused and again blinked his eyes before continuing. "Harry Gustafson was a very caring man. He worried about all of his staff, but particularly about John Gunner. He came to see me because of his growing concern regarding John's mental state."

Expecting a response, Wolfe looked first at Agent Christopher, then back at Agent Shuman as she finished making a note in her notebook. Both were waiting for him to continue. After a moment he did. "Several days ago the man left his van and all his equipment in the parking lot at the Senate Office Building and disappeared; for some time before that he had been demonstrating irresponsible behavior: acting strangely, imagining things that never happened, warning people of unspecified dangers. Because Mr. Gunner's job requires him to have numerous contacts within important government officials, Harry… Mr. Gustafson, was concerned that his condition could create problems. He wanted my thoughts about discharging him, or at least insisting he have a psychiatric evaluation - if and when he ever turns up that is. I agreed it would be a good idea."

"Sir..." Jane began after a thoughtful hesitation, "John Gunner seems to have had contact with Mr. Gustafson, Senator Anderson and Sheik al-Sameur shortly before each of them died from sudden heart attacks. Do you think there could be any possible connection between him and their deaths?"

Surprised by her question, Wolfe stiffened as she continued, "And could the TVNews agency be involved in any way?"

Obviously angered, Wolfe closed his file folder and got to his feet before replying. Then, looking down at her, in a stern tone of voice told her, "Agent Shuman, I cannot conceive of any possible relationship between a TV Cameraman and anyone's heart attack but if there is any connection that should be determined by you people, not by me."

"Yes sir, we're trying..." As Wolfe started away Jane asked one more question, "Sir, do you happen to know of a woman named Beryl Kinney?"

"No. Who is she? What does she have to do with this?"

Jane thought the look that flashed across Wolfe's face contradicted his answer. "I don't believe anything," she said, "But her name came up. I just thought you might have heard it."

"No. Don't know the woman." Wolfe turned and headed towards the door. Half way there he called over his shoulder, "I will ask Miss Harwood to give you the recording of John Gunner's call, and I will ask her to instruct Director Merrill to send the vice president and me daily reports about your progress with all this."

"Thank you Mr. Wolfe," Jane and Chris said in unison.

Well aware that comments and reactions were best kept to themselves until they left the building Jane and Chris were careful not to discuss the meeting until they reached their car. Then, as Chris settled into the driver's seat and clicked his safety belt, Jane let out a sigh of frustration and asked, "How much of what he told us do your believe?"

"Why wouldn't I believe him?"

"Come on Chris, you saw those little twitches. You know he wasn't telling us the truth about a lot of things."

"I can't argue with you." Equally frustrated, Chris banged both hands against the wheel. "There are too many things going on here: John Gunner warns the senator; John Gunner is a psychopath, John Gunner disappears; Harry Gustafson has a heart attack; John Gunner telephones Gordon. Wolfe; what's it all about?

"I don't know Chris, but I'm going to find out if it takes me forever."

"Forever may be a little extreme," Chris smiled, "But a bit of research might not be a bad idea. Where are you going to begin?"

"Well first of all I want to find out if there are any more dead bodies in John Gunner's past."

The Brentwood - Apt. 148

JANE SHUMAN stared at the notes she had assembled and hardly heard the soft voice of the all night music station announcer telling his listeners it was 2AM. After a long day at the office she had finally decided to grab a quick bite of dinner then continue her research at home. She had not anticipated the volume of material she would have to go through to track John Gunner's busy career. She was very good at research but there were times when she felt like a complete nerd searching through old files when other women her age were having dates with boyfriends or, as her mother was constantly reminding her, having babies. That was a life she sometimes thought about, more often these days than she used to. But then there were nights like tonight! Nights when her computer revealed secrets beyond belief. "Oh my god," she said with a sigh. Who could believe it? Why hadn't she researched this sooner? She couldn't wait for morning. She couldn't wait to get to the office and tell Chris what she had learned.

FBI Building

LESS THEN SEVEN HOURS later, in his usual courtly manner, David Christopher held the door for her then followed an obviously excited and bursting to tell all Agent Shuman as she almost ran into FBI Director Merrill's office.

"Good morning Jane, Chris…" the director stood to welcome them and nodded towards the chairs in front of his desk. "Sit down you two. Jane, you have that look on your face, I know you're about to drop a bomb shell and I don't know if I'm ready for bomb shells this morning."

"Sir, I think what Jane has turned up my really be a bomb shell ." Chris said as he held a chair for her.

The director's jovial mood changed quickly to one of serious concern, "Alright, what have you found?"

"Sir, this is about John Gunner," Jane answered. "I wanted to get some background information in case it might lead us to him…"

"Good thinking." The director nodded his head, "And what have you found?"

Jane opened the file folder she had brought with her. She did not often have an opportunity to report directly to the director so she was careful to use her most crisp, professional voice as she read from her notes: "Mr. Gunner began working at TVNews a little over four years ago. Being a government operation made it easy for me to click into the TVNews files where I found a listing of every assignment he ever had and, believe me, he was a working reporter so there were literally hundreds. I found four that may be of interest to us."

The director waited for a count of three before saying, "You have my full attention Agent Shuman…"

"Yes sir, sorry. Three years ago," she began slowly, "John Gunner was part of the press corps that traveled to Afghanistan with Assistant Secretary of State Morton. Along with two dozen or more photographers he covered a protest demonstration Rafik Assad conducted. Assad was reported to be one of the top terrorist leaders. While he was screaming curses about the U.S.A. Assad suddenly collapsed and died of a heart attack."

"Really."

"Yes sir." Jane nodded her head up and down. "Then, a little more than a year after that, Mr. Gunner went to Syria with the U.S. Trade Mission. Syrian Trade Minister Bashar Hariri was believed to be a Taliban leader. When Hariri arrived for a meeting, he stopped on a balcony to wave at the photographers. Suddenly he fell over the low railing and died. It was determined a heart attack caused his fall."

"Good lord. And there are two more?"

"Yes. A year ago, shortly after President Wadsworth died, Salam Faaheid, in Pakistan, and last month, Sheik al-Sameur, right here in DC.

"Wholly Shit!" The director's uncharacteristic profanity caused Jane to hesitate. "Sorry." He looked embarrassed. "Please, go on."

"Sir, I could not find any information tying either Faaheid or al-Sameur to terrorist activities, but both of them were very much involved with oil production." Jane looked up from her notes. Being the center of attention at a meeting in the Director's office was a bit unsettling, the look on his face was even more so. "Sir, Agent Christopher and I want to look at those videos."

"Of course, of course. You must do so at once." The director was silent for a moment. You could hear the proverbial pin drop, Jane thought. Then, almost in a whisper, he added, "Agent Shuman, you have done an excellent job."

"Thank you sir…"

Before she could say more Merrill picked up his telephone. "Miss Andrews, please find the Attorney General and put us through to him on a secure line." Director Merrill listened for a moment, said "Thank you," and returned the phone to its cradle.

"Agent Shuman," the Director focused his eyes on her. "When we reach the Attorney General, I will ask you to tell him exactly what you have just told me."

Moments later as Attorney General Jennings listened to Agent Shuman's report, he realized there was cause for serious concern. He had to admire her perseverance, but he knew the success she was having could have untold ramifications.

"Good work Agent Shuman," Jennings said when she completed her report. "I am most impressed by the research you have done. Please let me know immediately what you find when you look at Mr. Gunner's videos."

Unconsciously, Attorney General Jennings' fingers began drumming on his desk top as he switched off his phone.. What will happen when they find John Gunner? What will he tell them? What can he tell them? Almost everything, he realized. His fingers stopped drumming. He reached for his secure phone and punched in a number.

Silicon Valley, California

IN SPITE of being one of the wealthiest men in the country, if not the world, electronic genius, inventor of the "PRC Computer," PetRaCo founder, president, chairman of the board and majority stock holder, Arnold Petrakos, together with his wife Edith, lived a relatively simple life in the 25 room San Jose mansion that was their home. This morning, as on many mornings, Edith Petrakos herself had prepared the breakfast they were about to enjoy. Being a great believer in multi-tasking, husband Arnold was attempting to crack a soft boiled egg while paying almost full attention to his electronic newspaper when the phone in his shirt pocket began to vibrate. In spite of the surprise this caused he managed to successfully scoop the egg into a waiting cup without dropping it before looking towards his wife who was carefully spooning sliced strawberries on to her waffle.

"Sorry honey, I seem to be getting a call on my special." He put the phone to his ear, "Yes?..."

"Sorry to bother you this early Arnold," the voice he immediately recognized said, "But something has come up..."

Philadelphia

Gunner slept soundly 'till almost ten-thirty and blinked as he woke up; for a second or two he wasn't sure where he was. Philadelphia, he reminded himself as he swung his legs out of bed and headed for the shower. He had no razor so there was no question about shaving. Maybe he should re-grow his beard anyway. Would that be any help hiding his identity? Fuck! What good would it do? They have pictures of him with a beard and without one. He toweled himself dry then reached for his Tommy Hilfiger briefs and tee shirt. He had washed them before he turned in last night and they were still damp. "Last night," he chuckled, it was three o'clock in the morning, he reminded himself, no wonder they're not dry. But they aren't that wet and even if they were, they're all he had.

Lucas was behind the counter when Gunner came down stairs and called "Mornin' Marty." Then he glanced down at the registration book, "Or is it 'Ken' today?"

"I guess either one," Gunner grinned back as he walked to the desk. "I didn't really expect to see you again Lucas, but things being what they are…" he didn't finish the sentence.

"Yeah, I understand, and I got-a tell you, those are great pictures of you on TV."

"Ohhh damn," Gunner groaned. "You mean they're on here too?"

"Ten o'clock news. You're a real star."

"Christ. What am I gunna to do?"

"Plastic surgery might work," Lucas laughed.

"Thank you, Lucas. You're a really a great help."

"Well now maybe more than you think." He cocked an eyebrow and tried to look like a wise old owl. "Maybe if you were to go down and see Victor, tell him I sent you, he might have a couple of ideas about changing your looks a bit. Maybe not enough to fool those damn security computers, but enough to keep people from pointing you out."

"And do I assume Victor is in the beauty parlor downstairs?"

"Right as rain, which we seem to be having some of today," Lucas answered as he turned to reach into the corner next to the desk. A second later he produced an umbrella and handed it to Gunner. "Fella left this a while back. It's kind-a old, but it still works. You might find it handy."

"Thanks Lucas, appreciate it.".

"And while we're at it…" Lucas opened a drawer under the check-in counter and pulled out a heavy looking key. "You can spend a lot less time ducking our security camera if you use the fire stairs." He held out the key. "You know where the emergency door is on the back alley."

It was nearly noon when Lucas looked up to see the new John Gunner come through the Fire Exit door and walk towards him. "Jesus, Marty, your own mother wouldn't recognize you."

"Maybe not," Gunner agreed. "I'm not sure I recognize myself."

His nose was covered by a heavy bandage that was held in place by two, inch wide strips of adhesive tape extending half way across his cheeks. In addition, his hair had been cut to a length of not much more than half an inch. And there was something else,

Lucas didn't quite know what, but the shape of his face had changed, seemed somehow swollen.

"The bandage and the hair I can figure." Lucas shook his head from side to side, "But what did he do to your face?"

"Can't you tell by the way I'm talking?" Gunner wiggled his jaw around then produced one of the plastic pillows dentists sometimes use to keep patient's cheeks away from the area where they want to work. "Ingenious, huh?"

"Ingenious is right," Lucas agreed. "So now what?"

"I don't really know. Get out of here and find some place to lay low for a while until I can figure things out."

Actually he knew exactly where he was going and what he was going to do, but he didn't think anyone, not even Lucas, needed to know.

TVNews.Gov Office

THE ELEVATOR DOOR slid open and Special Agents Jane Shuman and David Christopher stepped into the reception lobby. Showing their badges and credentials to the slightly intimidated receptionist, Chris told the woman, "I'm Special Agent Christopher and this is Special Agent Shuman. We're here to see Mr. George Kline please."

"Yes sir. Mr. Kline's expecting you." As she spoke she picked up her phone and pressed the necessary buttons. "Mr. Kline, the FBI agents are here…."

Almost before the receptionist could hang up and tell the visitors, "Mr. Kline will be right out," Mr. Kline appeared.

"Hi. I'm George Kline."

Jane held out her hand. "Nice to meet you sir. I'm Special Agent Shuman and this is my boss, Special Agent David Christopher…" As the two men two men shook hands Jane asked, "Is there some place we can talk confidentially?"

"Sure, follow me." Kline led them to his office.

"This was Harry Gustafson's office, wasn't it?" Jane Shuman asked as they entered.

"Yes," Kline answered. "And I must tell you it feels a little uncomfortable... You know Harry was a pretty great guy, it isn't easy sitting in his office trying to fill his shoes. I'll be much happier when they appoint someone permanent to this job so I can go back to the news desk."

"I can appreciate that, Mr. Kline," Chris smiled, "May we sit down?"

"Yes, yes, of course." Obviously somewhat nervous, George Kline actually blushed slightly. "I'm sorry. Where are my manners?… Please do."

"We'll try not to take up too much of your time, Mr. Kline," Chris said as he held a chair for Jane Shuman to sit in.

"Mr. Kline," Chris began, "We still have no lead on where to find John Gunner and we are concerned something may have happened to him…"

"Jesus, I hope not," Kline interjected.

"We do too," Jane agreed. "Who was the last person to see him and when was that?"

"I guess it was Harry, the day he sent him off to Senator Anderson's office. That was before I came in. I don't know who else was around… I can ask?"

"Probably not necessary," Chris told him. "That was the last time he had contact with anyone at the office?"

"Yeah… well, no, Harry must have; he went over and picked up John's van. He didn't say anything about where John went though. He just said it was a personal matter and he would be gone for a few days."

"Something personal, not business?" Jane asked.

"Yes. That's what he said. If it was an assignment he would have taken his camera gear with him."

"And he didn't?" Jane asked.

"No."

As Jane made a note on her pad, Chris said, "I think when Agent Shuman telephoned she asked if we can see some of Mr. Gunner's videos…"

"The unedited material would be best," Jane added. "You never know, sometimes we can spot something or someone in the background or before the camera is turned off…"

"Yeah, sure," Kline smiled and got to his feet. "We keep a library of everything our cameramen shoot. World of computers you know, separate inventory for each man. Come on, there's a viewing room just down the hall, I'll set you up. All you got-a do is click on what you want to see."

George Kline switched on the monitor then handed the remote to Agent Christopher as the screen lit up. "Here you go. Probably two thousand or more stories chronologically listed there. You can skip to whatever you want. I'll leave you to it."

"Thank you, sir," Chris told the man then waited until he left the viewing room before asking Jane, "What's first?"

"Assignment number three hundred seventy-one."

Chris punched in the number and they sat quietly watching Rafik Assad ranting, screaming, shouting, then collapsing.

"God damn," Chris murmured as he looked away from the monitor. "What next?"

"Five eighty-eight," Jane told him.

Again silence as they watched Bashar Hann fall from the low balcony.

“Seven forty-three next,” Jane said. Salam Faaheid.

“Eight ninety-one.” Dulles Airport; al-Sameur.

“Chris, am I crazy or did each one of those men slap at something on his face just before he collapsed?”

“No, you are not crazy Jane. Each one of them was in a big closeup and each one seemed to be bothered by a bug or something…

“Chris,” Jane said very slowly. “It has to be his camera.”

“But he left his camera in the van. He didn’t have it when Senator Anderson died, or when Harry Gustafson did either,”

“I know.” Jane shook her head in agreement. “But I would like to take a look at the camera he used.”

“Find anything?” George Kline asked as Chris handed the computer remote back to him.

“No, I’m sorry to say,” Chris smiled, “But nothing ventured, nothing gained.

“Mr. Kline,” Jane jumped in, “Could we take a look at the camera Mr. Gunner was using?”

“Yeah, sure, if you want to.” Kline reached for his phone, “I’ll ask Tommy to bring it up. Tommy runs our camera department.”

“Oh, I’d love to see what a camera department looks like, can we just go there?” Jane asked.

“Sure, if that’s what you wanna do,” Kline put his phone back in its cradle. “Come on. Camera room’s down at the end of the hall.”

“Everybody’s got their own camera,” Tommy told them. “At least they think it’s their’s, they get real pissed if anybody else grabs the one they like. Only John’s actually was his own, not one of the company’s, so he never left it here with me.”

“We understand Mr. Gustafson brought Mr. Gunner’s van back from the Senate Office Building, wasn’t Mr. Gunner’s camera in it?” Chris asked.

“Yeah, it was. But Harry and John, you know they were pretty good pals and Harry wasn’t gunna let anyone mess around with John’s camera. He took it home with him.”

Jane pointed to the one video camera sitting on the shelf behind Tommy, “I notice that camera has the number 4 on it, do all your cameras have numbers?”

“Yes mam. We got five of ’em, numbered one to five.”

“What about Mr. Gunner’s camera, did it have a number?”

“No. Like I told you, it was his own camera. He put his initials on it, JG. Just under our logo.”

Baltimore, MD

EASTERN AVE. EXIT - 3 MILES. Gunner had not realized how hungry he was until he saw the sign. He was practically in Greek Town and he knew just the place to have lunch, Zorba's, on Eastern Avenue. He had been introduced to Zorba's a few months ago when he was sent to Baltimore to cover Representative George Newhouse's appearance at a big Greek Festival. The representative made a brief speech, shook a lot of hands and visited a lot of food stands but actually ate very little. Gunner found out why when it was time to leave: "Come on, John, you've been working hard following me around all afternoon now it's time for a little relaxation and some of the best food you will ever taste." Twenty minutes later he was introduced to Avgolemono Soup. He could not pronounce the name but the taste of the egg and lemon soup was wonderful. The thought of it made his mouth water and right now a bowl of that soup would be was just what the doctor ordered.

He had to remember to turn right when he came off 395, coming up from DC it had been a left turn, then only a few blocks up Eastern Avenue to the restaurant Parking was always a problem on Eastern Avenue. The second time around the block he spotted someone pulling out of spot just a few doors away from Zorba's. He parked, then checked his appearance in the rear view mirror. The bandaged nose and darker eyebrows were still intact. He had spit out the cotton dental cushions but he felt confident that with his Atlantic City fisherman's cap in place he would be safe from Security Central screening. The only problem might come from one of the waiters. Having been there with a local political hero it was possible someone might remember him. Was it a chance worth taking? Yes, he decided it was. He could be out of there quick enough if he was recognized. And even if he was recognized why would anyone there think to report him to the police?

The soup was every bit a good as he remembered. Just what he needed, something to eat and time to think. It had been his original thought to go all the way to DC and find a room to rent there but that was another fifty or so miles and with evening traffic beginning to build it would take him a couple of hours or more. So why not find a room here in Baltimore? That would make sense, he decided.

Soup finished he walked slowly back to the Subaru. Good old car, he clicked the door lock open and started to climb in when he noticed the hat in the window of the shop he had parked in front of. A cowboy hat. A ten gallon cowboy hat. He glanced at the name printed at the top of the shop window: "2nd Time Around." A wide brim like that could cover a lot of face and maybe they have some cowboy clothes too. Western ware would be very different from anything he ever wore before.

Washington, DC

"MR. HERMAN?"

"Yes. You must be…"

"Special Agents Shuman," Chris nodded towards his partner as they both held out their identification, "And Christopher, sir. Thank you for meeting us on such short notice."

Ira Herman, wearing a somewhat old fashion business suit complete with a vest and striped tie, was an elderly, cadaverously thin man. Late 60ies Jane Shuman thought as he courteously held the large, heavy looking front door to Harold Gustafson's home open and told them, "Yes, well I'm glad to help. Come in, come in."

A small foyer opened into a living room where comfortable leather furniture surrounded a real, wood burning fireplace. "Come," Herman continued as he led them into the room. "Have a seat and tell me what you are looking for."

Ignoring the suggestion to sit down, Christopher cleared his throat and in a somewhat formal tone of voice said, "Mr. Herman, you are Harold Gustafson's attorney and designated administrator?"

"Yes, that is correct."

"Then I will hand you this." Christopher took a search warrant from his inside coat pocket and held it out to the attorney. The ease with which they had obtained the search warrant troubled

Jane. As short a time ago as when she was in college it was still necessary to present some detailed information regarding the reason for a search to get a warrant, today they simply had to ask.

"Mr. Herman," Agent Christopher continued, "We are looking for a TVNews video camera that may have the initials 'JG' on it. The camera belonged to one of Mr. Gustafson's photo/reporters named John Gunner. We have been advised that following Mr. Gunner's disappearance Mr. Gustafson may have taken the camera. This warrant permits us to search this house and confiscate the camera if we find it." To anyone who did not know David Christopher as well as Jane did his actions would seem perfectly calm and natural, but she knew him too well to be deceived. Special Agent David Christopher was uncomfortable. Facing bad guys with drawn guns did not bother him in the least, but there was something about dealing with lawyers that always made him slightly nervous. She guessed it had to do with his concern about doing everything "by the book." Lawyers were always looking for some slight procedural slip-up to use as a reason for having a case thrown out of court.

Recognizing Christopher's discomfort, Ira Herman smiled as he accepted the paper, "Yes, well, the warrant has been properly served and acknowledged, Agent Christopher. Now if you look on the desk there in the den, I suspect you will find what you are looking for."

"Yes sir," Pulling on a pair of plastic gloves, Chris headed for the desk. "I suspect it is."

Reading the make, model and serial numbers while Chris held the camera up for her to see, Jane Shuman carefully noted the information on a receipt form then gave the original to Mr. Herman.

Afternoon traffic being what it was every Washington afternoon it was nearly six o'clock before they reached the FBI Lab and handed John Gunner's camera over to Technical Specialist Cecil

Lincoln. Less than half an hour after that Lincoln delivered his report:

“Finger prints all over it, most of ’em are your boy’s, but…” he shook his head slowly from side to side and held up the camera with John Gunner’s initials on it, “I don’t see anything unusual about the camera Jane, Chris. What am I supposed to be looking for?”

“Probably nothing,” Chris answered with a bit of a sigh. “We’re just on a little fishing trip.”

“Yeah, some days they just don’t seem ta bite.” Cecil shook his head in understanding. “Better luck next time.”

“Okay, Cecil, Thanks for everything.” Turning to Jane Shuman, Chris continued, “Time to go back to the office and do something productive.”

“What-a-ya want me to do with this?” Cecil pointed to the camera.

“I don’t know, log it in, hang on to it for a few days, then unless we can think of something better to do with it, I guess we’ll return it.”

“You got it, Chris. Good to see you both.”

Chris waited until they were outside the lab building before letting his disappointment get the better of him. “Damn-it! I really thought we were on to something.”

“We are, Chris. I know we are and I’m going to find out what.”

On Board PetRaCo G150 Gulf Stream

"WE ARE AN HOUR OUT, Mr. Petrakos."

Arnold Petrakos opened his eyes and looked up at the pretty face above him. "Ummm…" he blinked once or twice and stretched his shoulders as she pulled back the curtain. "Thank you Lori," he told her, then unhooking the safety belt he pushed back the blanket and swung his feet out into the aisle. "Nothing like an afternoon nap. What time is it?"

"Nearly five local time," she told him.

"Perfect. Let me wash my face then how about a snack. It's really lunch time back home."

"Ready when you are C.B."

Petrakos chuckled at her use of the old, old movie joke punch line. He doubted she or anyone her age had any idea who "CB" was or what the joke was all about. She just knew it was a line he frequently used. "Ah, to be young again," he said to himself. Not that he was so old, in today's world sixty was pretty young and he was in good shape "for the shape I'm in," he sometimes told himself. He was not a tall man but he stood straight and his regular exercise regimen kept his body well-toned. Women still found him attractive and, behind his back, men sometimes joked about him being plenty tall when he stood on his wallet.

"Good morning, boss. Have a nice nap?" Letting his co-pilot log some miles in the captain's chair today, Ron Chatsworth looked back from the co-pilot's chair as his boss made his way towards the well-appointed bathroom located just behind the cockpit

"Piss-off, Ronny," Petrakos managed a fake growl, "Just make sure you and the maestro there stay awake."

Forcing an exaggerated yawn, Chatsworth reached over and shook his co-pilot's arm, "Jack. You awake? Remember you can't really sleep in that chair, only snooze."

Petrakos couldn't keep from laughing, "Okay, I surrender." He had hired Chatsworth the day after the man received his discharge from the air force. During the six years since then they had become good friends. "How long we got left?" Petrakos asked.

Serious now, Chatsworth looked at the clock next to his head then answered, "Fifty three minutes to wheels down."

Petrakos nodded, told him, "Good enough," and went into the bathroom where washed the sleep out of his eyes then dropped his trousers and sat down on "the throne." Sometimes he did his best thinking while sitting on the throne and it was definitely time for some very serious thinking. Ever since Kempton's phone call he had been thinking the same thought: "How the hell did I get myself into this?" And, of course, he knew the answer perfectly well:

If he ever wrote a book he would title it, "The Curse of a Curious Mind." He had grown up curious with a love for physics and mathematics. While still in high school he had worked, scrimped and saved to buy one of the first microcomputer kits to come on the market. It was that computer and his curious mind that led to PetRaCo. It was that still overwhelming curiosity that led to his discovery of an electron bolt and a meeting with the President.

It begun several years ago when the Advanced Research Projects

Agency gave his company seed money to develop space weapons. As space weaponry and drone usage fell into Congressional disfavor the agency added the word "Defense" to its title. Then, as DARPA, the "Defense Advanced Research Projects Agency" it had abandoned many of its "Black Budget" projects, including his. But his curious mind would not let go and that curiosity led to the Graphene Supercapacetor Electron, and a radiation beam that could cause immediate, fatal heart failure. Since the GSE had grown from a DARPA project his first thought was to take it back there, but he'd had second thoughts - DARPA had Become synonymous with "Drones" and the growing controversy over drone usage had resulted in more and more Congressional Oversight. "Oversight" meant more and more people having more and more knowledge of its activities. In his mind the Electron Bolt should be kept as secret as possible. For that reason he had taken his discovery directly to President Wadsworth.

"My God, Arnold, do you think that thing can be perfected?" The President asked.

"I'm sure of it," he answered.

"Jesus! Do you realize what a weapon that could be?"

Indeed he did. Secretly, without "collateral damage," the Electron Bolt could partially replace drone strikes to eliminate people who were threats to the United States

"Arnold, you were right to bring this to me," the President told him. "Involving DARPA or any government agency would jeopardize its secrecy. If you can create a delivery system for it and finance the project, Attorney General Jennings and I will put together a very special unit to make use of it."

All had gone well until Wadsworth's sudden, unexpected death shortly after being re-elected to a second term.

Following Wadsworth's untimely death Vice President Helen

Langdon was sworn in as President of the United States. Helen Langdon was one of the very few, very trusted people to whom the President had imparted knowledge of Group 1, the Electron Beam and the need to use it wisely and, above all, the need to keep it secret.

Both he and the Attorney General had been concerned when President Langdon turned over control of Group 1 to her new Vice President and recent activity had greatly increased that concern. Neither Jennings nor himself believed there was justification for the elimination of Senator Anderson or Harry Gustafson. Would what he might learn during tomorrow's golf game change their minds?

Washington, DC

CARRYING HER BRIEFCASE and a handful of mail, mostly catalogues, in one hand and a bag of groceries along with her keys in the other, Jane Shuman stepped off the elevator, walked down the hall and managed to unlock her door without dropping a thing. Once inside, in an even more remarkable demonstration of manual dexterity, she somehow managed to switch on the hall light, kick the door closed and lock it before dumping the mail, her briefcase, and her keys on the hall table while still holding the bag of groceries which she then carried into the kitchen. Once in the kitchen, she turned on another light, put the grocery bag on the counter, then took a deep breath before pouring herself a glass of Rombauer Chardonnay. Rombauer was pretty expensive for an agent's salary but she didn't drink a lot, she spent very little money on clothes, and after a long day a glass of good wine was something she felt entitled to.

Leaving the groceries on the counter she carried the wine into her living room, put on some music and collapsed into her favorite arm chair. She leaned back, kicked off her shoes, and took a sip. "Oh Lord, that's good," she murmured. It had been an exhausting day; several days really, and they didn't seem to be any further ahead than they were a week ago. After a moment or two she took a second sip and told herself maybe she would just forget about dinner tonight, maybe the glass of wine was all she needed. The glass of wine and a good night's sleep, but sleep was out of the question for a while. After taking one more sip of wine she reluctantly put the glass on the end table, pulled her lap top onto her knees, and re-read Mark Winter's report on "the mystery woman" :

Beryl Kinney: Mother Canadian, father U.S. Citizen She has dual citizenship. Raised Port Washington, Long Island. Attended Long Island University. Computer Technology Degree. Employed United Airlines, NYC, one year. Joined FAA, NYC, two years ago. Last March transferred to DC. Attractive single young woman found herself living next door to single young man. They have dated several times. Seems like end of story.

At least one less worry she decided, worrying about John Gunner is more than enough, John Gunner and his tapes. Thanks to Norman Zight she could to take another look at Gunner's tapes right here in the comforts of her home, and this was much better than a second visit to George Kline's domain. As she watched and watched the tapes she became more and more convinced those deaths were in some way connected to John Gunner's camera. Yes, there were close up shots of other people sneezing, coughing, scratching, yawning, people doing any number of unconscious things, but none quite so deliberate - quite so definite - as the slap each of the four men had delivered to his cheek just seconds before death.

FBI Building

HOPING THE MORNING COFFEE she carried would help ward off the effects of an almost sleepless night Jane Shuman made her way to her desk and sank down into the comfortable chair behind it. “Oh, damn!” It burned her tongue. She tried to blow cool air through the tiny opening in the container cover then took a second sip. “Jesus!” Still too hot. It wasn’t until she set the container down to let it cool that she noticed the blinking message light. Norman Zight had called. Oh Lord, what does he want? She needed to talk with Chris about her conviction that Gunner’s camera had something to do with the deaths of the four men she watched collapse last night. But Norman was a friend and good at his job - she picked up her phone and clicked his number,

“Hi Norm. Good morning. What’s up?”

“Morning Jane. Listen, you know I spend half my life on my computer and I ran across something last night I thought might interest you. One of the people who found Harry Gustafson shot a lot of pictures and put them on Twitter. I sent them to you. Check ’em out.”

Jane tried to sniffle a threatening yawn as she answered, “Will do, Norm. Sounds verrry interesting. Thank you.” Picking up her coffee with one hand Jane switched on her computer with the other and watched as the material Norman had sent came up on the screen. Her reaction to the very first picture almost caused her to drop the still too hot to drink coffee. Bending over Harry Gustafson was one man in a sweat suit giving CPR, while a second man, with his hand on Gustafson’s shoulder, knelt next to the body. The second man had a camera hanging from a strap over his shoulder. Suddenly wide awake Jane grabbed her phone. It wasn't a movie camera, it was a still camera but cameras of any kind were becoming a fixation.

"Norm. It's me. Can you get a make on the man with a camera in the first picture?"

"I thought he might interest you." Jane could almost hear the smile in Norman's voice. "So I started looking. Trouble is you can see the camera pretty well but the man himself is mostly profile. I'll see what comes up, Jane, but don't hold your breath."

"Thanks Norm. I'll keep my fingers crossed."

Augusta, Georgia

"HIT AWAY ARNIE."

It had been many, many years since Arnold Palmer ruled the fairways but the name "Arnie" was still associated with him and Dex's use of it when they played golf together was usually a source of slight annoyance to Arnold Petrakos, but not today. Today, as he stepped up to the tee box, the need to talk with Dexter was his only concern. This concern, plus the light rain that was falling, resulted in him hooking his drive into the left hand rough.

"Oh my," the vice president chuckled as he placed his ball on his tee, "That may be out of bonds."

Without replying, "Arnie" handed his driver back to his caddy, climbed into the golf cart they shared, then watched Dexter hit, what was for him, a very good drive.

Vice President Dexter's love of golf was well known. His "second home" on the Augusta National Golf Course was often referred to as "the real summer white house" by cartoonists, and talk show comics, who took every opportunity to dismiss the "little woman in the White House" who had selected him.

In a world increasingly beset with energy problems, shortly after assuming the presidency, Helen Langdon had asked AllWorldOil's CEO and board chairman, Theodore Allan Dexter, to become her vice president. Much to the surprise of many people, Dexter, considered one of the most brilliant executives in the country, relinquished control of the international corporation he had built into one of the world's largest and most profitable and accepted President Langdon's invitation. Soon after that, never having been entirely comfortable with its "black" side although fully aware of its importance, in spite of contrary advice from Kempton Jennings and himself, President Langdon asked her new vice president to assume operational control of Group 1. That was when Arnold Petrakos' concerns about the unit began. Concerns that, according to the information Kempton had given him, were fully justified. Concerns that mandated this sudden trip to Georgia. He hoped the vice president could provide some believable explanations.

"Wat-a-ya think of that?" Dexter asked as he joined Petrakos. "Right down the middle."

"Frankly, Dex, I don't give a shit. Tell me about Orin Anderson and Harry Gustafson."

"Oh." Vice President Dexter's demeanor changed quickly as he looked back over his shoulder at the man riding "shot gun" on the back of the golf cart. "Dwight, we need to talk privately about some things. Give us a little room will you."

"Yes sir." The Secret Service man nodded his head up and down as he stepped off the cart.

"Arnie," Dexter spoke quietly as he started the cart down the fairway, "It was necessary, but there's too much to tell you about here. Let's play a few holes then go over to your place and have a drink."

Through three holes of play the vice president made no further mention of the situation that was causing his partner increasing distress. Finally, as they reached the fourth hole and the light drizzle Dexter had insisted was, "Not really rain," turned into a steady down pour, Arnold's patience reached an end. "Enough of this shit," he growled in disgust, "We need to talk."

“Okay, good,“ the vice president agreed.

Petrakos punched numbers into his phone and a moment later said, “Hi Rico. Vice President Dexter and I are going to shoot some pool and have a couple of drinks in the game room. Put a fire in the fireplace and see if you can find some glasses, ice and a bottle of bourbon, the cheap stuff,” he added with a forced chuckle. “We’ll be there as soon as we can get out of these wet clothes.”

Arnold Petrakos’ sixteen room “cottage” on Vineland Avenue, opposite the Augusta Golf Course, was modest compared to the vice president’s home further up the street, but it was comfortable and boasted a handsome game room complete with a small bar, a large fireplace, comfortable chairs, sofas, and best of all, a perfectly balanced pool table. “Billiard Table,” Arnold’s wife laughed whenever he mentioned it, “Pool table sounds so very common,” she usually added in her pseudo socialite voice.

Whenever the vice president and Arnie Petrakos were together in Augusta they seldom missed the fun of 8-Ball and bourbon in Petrakos’ game room. None the less, each time they ventured there, Dwight Zimmerman, the Secret Service Agent in Charge of the vice president‘s security, insisted the visit be preceded by a security check of the building. This rainy afternoon was no different.

“Jesus Dex,” Petrakos groaned as they sat waiting in the vice president’s limo, “It’s like they don’t trust me.”

“It’s not you Arnie, It‘s just regulations. Wait ‘till you see what they do to your place in Pebble Beach.”

“Pebble Beach?” Petrakos blinked. “What have you got in mind for Pebble Beach?”

“Oh,” the vice president laughed. “I guess I didn’t tell you. I’m gonna play in that “First Tee” tourney out there on 4th of July weekend. I sort of invited myself to stay at your place. I'll bring my own bourbon, he added with a laugh."

"Okay, fine, I don't really care Dex. What I care about is Harry Gustafson and Orin Anderson. Now let's try to stay focused on that. Can we?"

Before the vice president could respond, Agent Zimmerman opened the car door to announce, "All clear sir."

Racked balls on the pool table, a cheery fire in the fireplace, and houseman Rico Morales waiting with glasses, ice, and a crystal decanter filled with whisky, welcomed the two men. Pointing towards the Waterford glasses Petrakos said, "Couple-a inches each please Rico, then beat it out of here. We'll probably want some lunch later but right now Vice President Dexter and I want to tell dirty jokes." Nothing like a chuckle and a grin to hide serious thoughts, Petrakos assured himself as he watched a smiling Rico carefully pour the specified amount of thirty year old bourbon into each glass, add three cubes of ice, then hand one to the vice president and the other to him. Replacing the decanter stopper, Rico quickly checked the fire in the huge river-stone fireplace, then bowed slightly and hurried out of the room.

"Here's to playing a full eighteen someday," the vice president laughed as he lifted his glass.

"Screw that, Dex. Let's get serious."

"Ummm." The vice president's groan was clearly audible, "I guess we need to." He slowly put his glass to his lips and took a long sip before continuing. "Arnold, I know you're upset about the way things have been going and I am too, but not for the same reasons."

"What exactly does that mean Dex?"

"It means..." The vice president hesitated, "Arnie, I'm sure you know the president and I have access to a number of highly secret, very confidential information sources."

Petrakos nodded his head but did not make a verbal response...

"A few weeks ago I received information regarding Sheik al-Sameur and his relationship with Orin Anderson. I found it hard to believe, but the sheik's visit here was to secure information from Anderson and, with him, set up attacks on our country's financial stability. I'm not sure Helen is tuned in to all this, she leaves a lot of things in my hands, but it was an immediate threat Arnold. We had to act quickly. The sheik was easy. Making sure Anderson had gone over took a bit longer, but when I was certain, I gave Gordon instructions to resolve the situation."

It was Petrakos' turn to take a thoughtful sip of bourbon before making any comment. Then, "You're right, Dex. Very hard to believe." He took a second sip before adding, "And what about Harry Gustafson? Surely he wasn't planning an attack on our financial system."

"A much more devastating attack than that, Arnold. An agent named John Gunner was originally given the Anderson assignment. He disobeyed the order and ran away. Gustafson had been insisting Gunner was loyal. He threatened to go to the FBI and reveal the existence of Group One unless Gunner was immediately reinstated." Dexter fixed his eyes on Petrakos', "Gustafson had to be eliminated! I'm upset because Gordon arranged it without consulting me and stupidly ordered another heart attack." The vice president finished his bourbon in one long sip before adding, "I'm concerned about Gordon."

"Really?" Petrakos asked.

"Really," Dexter bowed his head slightly and began to massage his forehead with the fingers of his left hand. "Gordon's a good man," he said slowly, "Loyal and devoted, but sometimes he makes very poor decisions and I'm not certain how he'll act under pressure."

"What pressure would that be?" Petrakos asked.

"FBI pressure," Dexter answered. "Two agents met with him yesterday. Right now they're looking for John Gunner. If they find him before we do, God knows what he might tell them. No matter, sooner or later they're going to want to talk to Gordon again. They know Harry was Gunner's boss and if they don't already know, they'll find out Harry had breakfast with Gordon the day before he died."

"You think Gordon will tell them something about G One?"

"No, no not at first," Dexter grimaced, "But you know the fucking FBI, like a dog with a bone, they never quit chewing away. I don‘t know how long Gordon will stand up to that."

Twenty minutes after the vice president left, Arnold Petrakos telephoned Attorney General Kempton Jennings and from the tiny, undetectable devices installed in the Waterford glasses in which Rico had served them, played a recording of his conversation with the vice president.

"What do we know about al-Sameur and Orin Anderson?" Arnold asked when the recording ended.

"Enough to be reasonable certain the sheik was coming here to give Anderson's committee some first-hand knowledge about AllWorld's sponsoring the on-going wars in his country," Jennings answered.

"And Harry Gustafson? You think he would blow Group One?"

"Never!"

For several seconds neither man spoke, then Arnold Petrakos said, “I don’t believe Group One was created for this kind of activity, Kempton.”

“Nor do I, Arnold. I need to discuss it with the president.”

“Yes. Hard to believe she doesn’t know what’s going on.”

“She may know more that you think.” The attorney general’s tone of voice became a bit stronger, “Don’t sell her short Arnold. I‘ll talk with her as soon as I can.”

“Okay. Let me know what she has to say. I’m going back home, things I need to do.”

Office of the Attorney General

KEMPTON JENNINGS had hardly switched off his phone when his secretary's voice advised him, "Director Merrill on line three…"

"Thank you," the attorney general told the intercom as he reached for the telephone.
"Wilson, how nice to hear from you. How is Stephaney feeling today?"

"Oh she's much better Kempton. Thanks for asking."

"No thanks necessary, please give her my best…"

"I'll do that. She'll be happy to know you asked about her."

"Very good. Now, what's on your mind?"

"Quite a bit, Kempton. A lot's been happening on the John Gunner front…"

The attorney general listened without comment as Director Merrill meticulously reported the results of Agent Christopher's and Agent Shuman's viewing of John Gunner's tapes and subsequent examination of Gunner's camera.

"My God, Wilson, what an idea." Jennings said when Merrill concluded his report, "But the camera is perfectly normal?"

“Yes, apparently. And speaking of cameras, Gordon Wolfe’s office has received two more phone calls from John Gunner insisting Harry Gustafson ordered him to take Wolfe’s picture.”

“Really. What do you make of that/”

“I don’t know Kempton but we are going to find out. Both calls came from the Baltimore area. We have an A-Plus alert there.”

“That sounds good Merrill. Let me know the minutes you find him or learn anything new.” The Attorney General returned his telephone to its cradle then quickly picked it up again to call president‘s office. It was time he filled her in. She would see him in twenty minutes. He glanced up at the antique grandfather clock standing against the wall opposite his desk. Almost three -thirty, the chimes would ring in a moment.

Oval Office - White House

"IT IS VERY GOOD of you to see me on such short notice, Madame President."

"Kempton you know perfectly well there is no one on earth more welcome in this office any time, day or night, short notice or none." The president's broad smile as she rose from behind her desk to greet her visitor gave visible proof of the sincerity of her words. "Now come sit down and tell me why you're here."

"Thank you Madam President…" The attorney general stepped to the side as President Langdon made her way past him to one of the two sofas and waited until she sat down before taking a seat opposite her.

"…And you can stop the 'Madam President' business, Kempton. We are all alone here."

"Yes, all right Helen, thank you." Easing himself back into the comfortable cushions, Jennings lowered his voice slightly, "Helen, I need to talk with you about a matter of considerable delicacy. If you have recording devices working it would be best to turn them off."

"I never record what you and I talk about, Kempton. You know that."

"Yes… yes, I guess I do. And I appreciate it…"

"Kempton, you seem a bit reluctant to get down to whatever it is you came to talk about."

“I suppose I am,” he said slowly. Then… “Helen I’ve come to talk to you about Group One,” he said at last. Other than for a quick intake of breath the president showed no reaction to Jennings’ announcement. “The recent deaths of Sheik al-Sameur, Senator Orin Anderson, and TVNews Director Harry Gustafson were almost certainly the results of Group One activity.”

“Jesus Christ, Kempton.” The president’s un-blinking eyes were riveted on him, “How did you come up with that idea?”

In calm, carefully chosen words, the attorney general gave the president a detailed report on Arnold Petrakos’ meeting with the Vice President, the John Gunner situation, and the investigation headed by Special Agents Jane Shuman and David Christopher. “Somehow, Harry Gustafson must have replaced Gunner’s camera, but Shuman and Christopher are convinced there is a secret weapon in existence,” Jennings continued, “And they are determined to find it.”

“Do you think that’s possible Kempton?”

“Yes I do. They’re smart and diligent and sooner or later they are going to find John Gunner; when they do… well, who knows? I don’t believe Gunner would deliberately give them any information but, you know, they are damn clever. People sometimes tell them things they don’t mean to and revealing anything about Group One and that weapon could have very serious repercussions, not just here in our country but throughout the world.”

“I am well aware of that, Kempton.” The president got up from her seat opposite him and walked to her desk where she stood looking up at the American Flag behind it. The decision to permit the continued existence of Group 1 had been perhaps the most difficult one she had to make during those first trying days after Franklin Wadsworth’s death until, in a moment of amazing clarity, she realized there was really no decision to make. The weapon existed. That genie was out of the bottle. Since time began, once a new weapon was invented it never went away, it just got bigger, more powerful, more devastating; no one could ever put it back in the bottle.

When the President first told her of Group 1 and the Electron Bolt she had asked why the project was not turned over to DARPA.

"First of all," Wadsworth had answered, "The research is done. Arnold has done it. Secondly, DARPA involvement would mean more people would know our secret and the more people who know, the more chance there is of a leak."

She had accepted his logic. She was far too much of a realist to believe anything could be kept secret forever, but until someone else found the secret, or stole it, the Graphene Supercapacetor Electron. belonged to the United States alone, to use against its enemies in defense of its sovereignty. The only thing she could do was hold on to it and keep it secret for as long as possible. Group 1 had the weapon and the President controlled Group 1. But this was not completely true, she reminded herself. First off, it is really Arnold Petrakos who controls Group 1. Or at least he controls the funding and the produces weapon used by Group 1 and that gave him the ultimate control - a situation which she knew in time needed to be changed. None the less, when she became President she gained the power to quietly, secretly eliminate individual enemies as she saw fit. It was, however, a power with which she had not been comfortable.

She had asked Ted Dexter to become her Vice President because of his vast knowledge of world affairs gained through his brilliant management of AllWorldOil. Once sworn in, she had revealed the existence of Group 1 to him and her discomfort at exercising the power it gave her; Dexter had offered to be a "buffer," offered to handle the control of Group 1. She had accepted his offer. Now, what Kempton was telling her seemed to bear out a suspicion that had been growing in her mind, a suspicion that the Vice President was not the person to whom she should have given that responsibility.. Were she to be faced with such a situation today, she would make a very different decision.

That, she knew, was the result of her "on-the-job" training. She was a far different person today than when Franklin died. She was no longer an idealist. Today she knew that intrigue and deception were an important part of political life; an essential part of political life, a part with which she was becoming more and more proficient.

After what seemed a very long time to the attorney general, the president turned back to look at him again. "Are you convinced the Vice President is responsible for all this?"

"Yes Helen, I am."

"Gordon Wolfe as well?"

"Yes. I believe he was only carrying out orders, but he was fully involved."

"What about John Gunner? What about his phone calls to Gordon?"

After a brief hesitation the attorney general answered. "It's a bit like Humpty-Dumpty, Helen. Gunner fell off the wall… more correctly he was pushed off. He tried to do the right thing by not eliminating Orin Anderson, but now he's odd man out and he doesn't know how to put the pieces together again. I'm certain he knows Harry Gustafson met with Wolfe in an effort to have him reinstated and Wolfe turned him down. I suspect he believes Wolfe was then responsible for Gustafson's death and is seeking retribution. What he expects the phone calls to do is beyond me."

"None the less, he has the knowledge and the equipment to reveal everything about Group One?"

"If he has a mind to," Jennings agreed, "But, as I said, I don't believe he will do so intentionally. If that was his intention he could have done so when he was given the order to eliminate Orin Anderson. No Helen, I think he is trying to punish Gordon Wolfe and at the same time save his own skin."

That seemed in accordance with other information she was gathering. Information from sources not even Kempton Jennings was aware of. "And the other field agents," she asked after a moment. "I believe there are two others?"

"Yes."

"What is your feeling about them?"

The attorney general took a deep breath before answering. Then, with his head slightly nodding up and down he spoke, "I think they are loyal to the unit. I think they will do whatever they are told to do without question."

"I see." Again deep in thought, the president closed her eyes while the attorney general sat quietly waiting for her to continue; when she did it reminded him of how wrong people were in believing she was afraid of making tough decisions.

"I will advise the Vice President that Group One must go on hiatus immediately. We must not lose the technology but the unit must go into the deep freeze and stay there for a while."

"I agree…"

"Good." Helen Langdon's face took on an even more serious expression. "With respect to John Gunner, I leave that on the table for the moment. As for the Vice President and Gordon Wolfe, those problems must be eliminated as quickly as possible." The president's eyes bore into the attorney general, "Can this be discretely accomplished?"

"Yes," the attorney general nodded his head up and down, "I believe so, Helen."

Petrakos Research - San Jose, CA

"WELCOME BACK, Mr. Petrakos," the surprised receptionist smiled a pretty smile, "Didn't expect to see you back here today."

"Things to do, Dianna," he tried to return her smile. "No rest for the weary, besides it's still early."

"Yes sir, but in Georgia it's eight o'clock, or is it six? I can never remember."

"In that case you probably belong over in Shipping. They never seem to know what day it is, let alone what time."

"Oh that would be fun. There's lots of cute boys over in Shipping," she smiled an even prettier smile, "But movie producers might not see me there. I'd better stay here. And I really know it's five o'clock in Georgia… or is that in Chicago?"

Petrakos shook his head and rolled his eyes, "Jesus, you are really hopeless Di." He started towards the elevator, "Now see if you can figure out how to let Norma know I'm back."

"I wouldn't mind having her job," Dianna called after him.

Norma had already been alerted to the boss' arrival by the three short beeps Di signaled to her when he walked into the building. While he was chatting with Dianna, then elevatoring to the 3rd floor, Norma switched on his office lights, plugged in the coffee maker and checked to see that everything was ready for his arrival.

"Well, did you break par?"

"No, Norma I did not break par and by the way, how would you like to switch jobs with Dianna?"

"Oh, ouch. In the nineties, huh?"

Turning to face his assistant directly, Petrakos lifted his arm and pointed his finger towards the door in a pretty good imitation of an old black and white movie tyrant, "Go! Never darken my doorstep again."

Hanging her head and wiping an imaginary tear from her eye, Norma did an equally good imitation of the tormented young heroine as she headed out of the office muttering, "Oh my God… over a hundred…".

With a grin on his face Arnold Petrakos watched his bright, attractive assistant tearfully close the door to his office before typing a pass word into his computer. There was only one other computer in the world with similar capabilities… almost similar capabilities; the computer he had designed for, and installed at, Computer Central in Washington, DC. The only significant difference between the two being that, unbeknown to anyone, his computer could override the one in Washington, DC. He waited the brief few seconds it took to boot up, then his grin turned into a look of determination. It would not be good to have the FBI locate John Gunner. No matter what action Kempton and the president might decide on, he felt certain there would come a time when John Gunner could be very useful. A few clicks removed Gunner from Security Central purview. A few more clicks installed a search for him on his own computer. He was confident sooner or later he would turn up. That done he clicked on his incoming mail. There was just one message:

"Can we go fishing tomorrow?"

It took only seconds to reply: "Yes."

Washington, DC

AROUND THE WEST WING they were known as "the M&M's": Marion Harwood and Mildred Thomas, secretary/assistants to the chief of staff and the vice president respectively. Because of their important, and confidential positions, the "M&M's" did not much fraternize with other members of the vice president's staff, nor anyone else for that matter. It was only during their "at least once a week" luncheons at Lilly's that the two had time to let their hair down and talk of many things. There, over Cobb salads, or perhaps delicate salmon/broccoli quiches, along with glasses of a lovely French Sauvignon Blanc, Marion and Mildred confided in one and other about the trials and tribulations that elevated stress levels for themselves and their very important bosses. Today it was Marion who dominated their conversation:

"…And if that weren't enough," Marion rolled her eyes and shook her head as she continued in a half whisper, "This morning we had another phone call from him talking about taking Mr. Wolfe's picture with a new camera he got from poor Mr. Gustafson. The man must be completely insane…"

Weekly luncheon forgotten, a slightly harried Mildred Thomas was busy taking notes and collecting papers from her boss. It was always extra busy when he first returned from his golf outings in Georgia. As she bustled about she happened to express her relief that, "At least we don't have all that TVNews business to deal with."

"What business is that?" Vice President Dexter asked.

"Oh my goodness, visits from the FBI and phone calls from some crazy TV Cameraman wanting to take Mr. Wolfe's picture Marion was telling me what a nuisance it all is."

Despite the hackles that rose on the back of his neck, the vice president managed a chuckle, "Better them than us I suppose, but I should probably find out just what's going on. Ask Gordon to come over…"

His concern for Gordon Wolfe's activities was growing. Phone calls from John Gunner and FBI questionings were not good. And this Beryl Kinney business, he reminded himself. Who the hell is she? He waited until Mildred left the office before again reading Martin Small's report about Beryl Kinney. Why in God's name did Gordon bring NSA into this? His thoughts were interrupted by a knock on his door followed by the entrance of his Administrative Assistant, C. Gordon Wolfe.

"You wanted to see me?"

"Yeah, sit down Gordo, we need to talk."

Big Wood River Valley, Idaho

SOME TWENTY-FIVE MILES north of Ketchum, Idaho, fed by snow melt from the mountains surrounding 11,000 foot high Galena Peak as well as from frequent summer rains, any number of mountain streams come together to form the Big Wood River; a river of unusual beauty that winds its way past Sun Valley, Ketchum, Hailey and other small towns that make up Idaho's most tourist attractive valley; an area that invites skiers in the winter, golfers in the summer, fisherman and outdoor people all year round. Although the Big Wood River is highly touted in recreation advertising as a leading trout fishing stream, natives know this designation is highly over rated, a fact that does nothing to dissuade visitors and locals from frequently "wetting their lines" regardless of the likelihood, or lack thereof, of catching a fish. Such activity is particularly common to those fortunate few who live, usually part time, along the banks of the Big Wood. And, if the truth be known, few of these fishermen are anxious to catch trout anyhow; for it is not fish they seek while wading in the crystal clear stream of water, it is the absolute joy of being outdoors in one of God's most beautiful places.

Kempton Jennings arrived at Hailey's very active airport less than half an hour before the Petrakos jet landed. After a warm hand shake the two men climbed into a waiting SUV in which Jennings' houseman, Loren White, would drive them to what Jennings always referred to as "my cabin," a handsome 11 room lodge, on the river, just north of town. Once there, hurrying to catch the "evening rise," both men quickly donned fishing gear and walked the fifty or so yards from the lodge's front patio to the river's edge where, for the next hour, each tried several different fly patterns with virtually no success. Jennings actually "turned one over," but other than for that neither accomplished anything more than relieving stress and thoroughly enjoying the serene beauty of their surroundings.

"I have fished most assiduously," the attorney general announced at last. "Now I believe it is time to enjoy one of Loren's excellent martinis."

"I suppose there could be worse things to do," Arnold Petrakos agreed. He was always surprised by how quickly it cooled off once the sun got behind the mountain just in back of Jennings' house. Twenty minutes ago, standing in the sunshine, he had been almost too warm; now the thought of relaxing in front of a fire burning in the big, stone, living room fireplace was very appealing.

"Ah, thank you Loren," Jennings raised his glass and nodded to his guest, "Here's to better luck next time." Then, turning back to his young house man after taking an exploratory sip, "Excellent as ever my boy. Now you better be off or that lady friend of your's will never forgive me."

"Yeah, you don't want her mad at you," Loren laughed. "You sure you don't need anything else before I go?"

"No. We will be just fine Loren. Have fun."

Petrakos smiled and waved his glass towards the departing houseman. Sooner or later, he was sure, Kempton will get around to what he wants to tell me, meanwhile the martini is very enjoyable.

Waiting until Loren closed the living room door behind him as he left, Jennings held up his martini glass so he could look through the drink at the fire burning in the fireplace, then began, "Let me tell you what has been going on…"

Suddenly Arnold Petrakos was totally alert.

"Two very competent FBI agents have been looking into John Gunner's background. They have viewed his tapes and decided he has some kind of weapon capable of causing heart failure, possibly his camera."

Arnold's groan was loud enough to cause Jennings to pause, then continue, "They located what they believe is Gunner's camera, but it isn't. Somehow Harry must have got rid of Gunner's camera and substituted another, but these two agents are smart and determined, sooner or later they are going to…."

"I get the picture, Kempton," Petrakos interrupted. "And what does the president have to say about all this?"

"I gave her a complete rundown on your meeting with the vice president and she agrees Dexter and Gordon Wolfe have been using the unit for personal, non-sanctioned purposes. She wants that problem eliminated as soon as possible. Until it is, she wants the unit put, 'on ice', as she phrased it." Jennings hesitated before adding, "I assured her Hunter and Savage are not part of the problem. I have no doubt they will do anything they are asked to do, but about John Gunner I'm not so sure. The repeated phone calls to Gordon Wolfe concern me. He's been outside for too long, sooner or later the FBI is going to find him, and he could reveal the existence of the electronic bullet if he chooses to do so." Jennings drained his glass before adding, "This is a mess that must come to an end."

Petrakos leaned forward in his chair and asked, "Do you have in mind some way to do that?"

Jennings slowly put his empty glass down on the table next to him as he said, "The president and I are hoping you may Arnold."

Cypress Gallery - Manhasset, N.Y.

STEPHEN HUNTER blinked as he looked at the now dead phone in his hand. What a way to start the day. It wasn't that he did not understand what the metallic voice had ordered, it was just that he was surprised by it. Then again, maybe not so surprised. Things had not been going well lately, recent assignments were hard to understand: the senator and the colonel. Perhaps those were the reason for this. He punched the intercom button.

"Sir?"

"See if you can get me on a flight to DC this afternoon please Ethel."

"Yes sir, right away."

"Thanks."

Washington, DC

JOHN GUNNER"S frustration level had reached a point where some action, any action, was preferable to doing nothing. He was certain Gordon Wolfe was responsible for the colonel's death but phone calls to Wolfe's office were not accomplishing anything. "What did you expect them to accomplish?" He asked himself. He shook his head, he didn't know. Something in the back of his mind kept telling him his calls would cause at least a small amount of concern, would cause Wolfe to look over his shoulder once in a while, would make him feel uncomfortable, and people who have concerns, who feel uncomfortable sometimes do foolish things. "Yeah? Like what?" He wondered. Good question. Fuck-It! The hotel was just a block away. When Wolfe learns he had been right there where he lives… Well, it should stir up a little more concern, but in the long run it would be up to him. He would have to take action. He would have to exact retribution.

"I'm sorry sir, no parking here, the valet will take your car." The last thing the Woodland Park would want to have in front of the entrance was a ten year old Subaru Forester but a ten dollar bill convinced the doorman it would be okay to leave it for just a moment while he left something at the front desk. Probably he could have given the envelope to the doorman and probably it would have gotten to Gordon Wolfe but Gunner wanted to be certain and he had enough confidence in his "Cowboy" outfit to believe a quick visit to the lobby desk would be safe. *"Hi Gordon. I'm here and ready to take your picture."* The note inside the envelope read. *"Can we get together for breakfast?"*

"Yes sir, I'll see to it that Mr. Wolfe gets this," the desk clerk assured him.

“Thank-ya mam,” Gunner told her in what he considered to be a western drawl. Two minutes later he retrieved his keys from the doorman and climbed back into the Forester. He clicked in his seat belt, turned on the ever faithful engine, switched on his turn signal and was about to pull away from the curb when a taxi cab pulled up in front of him. “Son of a bitch!” He said out loud. The temptation to get out and tell the taxi driver what he thought of him was there but common sense told him calling attention to himself that way would be a dumb thing to do.

The hotel doorman was quick to open the taxi door and Gunner could hear him welcome the arriving guest. “Good evening Mr. Hunter.” It wasn’t until the man was out of the cab that Gunner could see him clearly. Jesus Christ! Mr. Hunter was the man from Starbucks. And the man from Starbucks was looking directly back at him. There seemed to be no sign of recognition on his face. Was there a reflection in the windshield that prevented him from seeing who was in the Forester? Did the ten gallon hat make recognition impossible? Or was the man from Starbucks just so damn good at his job that he was able to completely conceal any sign of recognition as he turned his attention back to the doorman?

The taxi pulled away. Gunner followed it out the driveway while trying to keep an eye on his rear view mirror. As far as he could tell there still no reaction from the man.

The quick glance was all Stephen Hunter needed to know the fellow in the cowboy hat was John Gunner. Dealing in fine art had helped him develop an ability for immediate visual recognition. Spotting a valuable piece of art without revealing to the dealer his interest in it could save him hundreds, sometimes thousands of dollars. Spotting a target could earn him even more. But John Gunner was not today’s assignment. He would report seeing him here in Washington; here at Gordon Wolfe’s home no less. But finding him again would not be easy. He had no idea where John Gunner might have gone. He had no ability to follow him. Okay, locating him was not his job anyway. Location was G1's job. Elimination was his.

"Who's the cowboy?" Hunter asked as he handed a five dollar bill to the doorman.

"No idea Mister Hunter. Said he had to deliver something to the front desk and would just be a moment."

Woodland Park Hotel

IT WAS SIX MINUTES to three o'clock in the morning when the DC Police car arrived. "Jesus, you guys got here quick!" Richard Zwerline told the two officers as he held the main entrance door open for them.

"Gun shots at a place with your kind of guest list gets quick attention," one of the two officers told him. "Where are we?"

"Just one shot," Zwerline answered. "East Tower, top floor, C. Gordon Wolfe's apartment."

"C. Gordon…? No shit," the second officer muttered as they headed for the elevator. "Let's go look."

A second police car arrived before the elevator door closed and Zwerline held it open while two more officers joined them.

In spite of the early morning hour several bathrobe wearing men were gathered in front of Wolfe's apartment door. "Gentlemen, please," the lead officer, a sergeant, said softly, "I would appreciate it if you will all return to your rooms. We're going to open this door in a moment and we don't want you exposed to any possible danger." As he spoke, with outstretched arms, two of the three other officer gently urged the men to move away from the door. "Thank you, thank you gentlemen. We don't want anyone hurt here."

As the would be spectators reluctantly moved away, the sergeant knocked on the apartment door, waited a half minute then rapped again. There was no sound from inside. Drawing his revolver from its holster he looked to Zwerline, "All right, Rich, gimme the key."

The foyer seemed to be dark. Listening, the officers waited for several seconds before entering. Once inside they could see a bit of light coming from a room down the hallway. The light turned out to be a lamp on C. Gordon Wolfe's desk. C. Gordon Wolfe himself was slumped over the desk, a pool of blood collecting next to his head, a revolver lying next to his lifeless hand.

Baltimore, MD

WAKING UP to unexpected news was getting to be a common factor in John Gunner's life and this morning's news was certainly unexpected. Gordon Wolfe - a suicide. Is it possible his phone calls and yesterday's note were responsible? Yes, he quickly decided, yes, they had to be a factor. Okay, the assignment he had given to himself was completed, now what? Did Wolfe's death cancel out G1's John Gunner Assignment or would the man named Hunter still be looking for him, still be seeking an opportunity to eliminate him? Without Gordon Wolfe was there still a Group One? Could he be reinstated? How could he find out? Questions. My God there were so many questions and he had no idea where to find answers. Well, not here anyway. Not in Baltimore.

FBI HEADQUARTERS

"I DON'T BELIEVE it was a suicide, Chris, I don't care what the police think, I think he was murdered. The police did a lousy job," her voice gave evidence of her frustration, "They just assumed it was a suicide and walked away from it."

"All right, Jane. Easy girl." He waited a few beats before continuing. "Now exactly what is it that makes you so certain it wasn't a suicide?"

Her eyes flashed as she asked, "You wanna know in one word?"

"That would be good," he answered.

"C. Gordon Wolfe was left handed and he was shot on the right side of the head."

Special Agent Christopher's eyes widened, "Not exactly one word, but very interesting. How do you know he was left handed?"

"Because when we interviewed him he made notes with his left hand."

"And you don't think someone who is left handed can shoot himself on the right side of his head?"

"Listen, Chris, anything's possible, but damn-it-all, it ought to raise a couple of eyebrows. It ought to produce a little more detective work than it has."

"So you think he was murdered?"

Jane looked intently at her boss. "You tell me Chris. What-a you think?"

David Christopher sat silently for a long moment before answering, "I think it could be murder… and I would like to know where John Gunner was last night."

"I'd like to know that too. And I want the DC police to really look into this."

"You know they are not too happy about having us look over their shoulder," he reminded her.

"Well maybe we can stimulate them to a little activity on their own. I for one am curious…"

"…To know what they might find," Chris jumped in to finish her sentence.. "Any thoughts on how to do that?"

"I don't know…" the hint of a smile crossed Jane's face, "Maybe."

"Yes, Jane?"

"Yes, what?" .

"What are you thinking?"

The slight smile turned into a look of sweet innocence, "Oh, nothing really."

"Nothing my ass! I know you better than that. Now what the hell are you thinking about?"

"Well if you must know, Chris, I have a dinner date this evening, and right now I'm just thinking about what to wear."

"Bull shit!"

Restorante Tosca - Washington, DC.

"I'M GOING TO HAVE the spaghetti with clam sauce," Jane Shuman told the waiter as he poured a bit more Pinot Grigio into her glass. The outdoor patio at Restorante Tosca was definitely one of her favorite places to dine and had been ever since Alvin Hamel introduced her to it.

"You wanna-da red sauce or da white?"

"Oh the white, Jane answered. "Definitely the white."

The waiter gave an approving smile and told her, "At's-a da best," as he turned to Alvin for his order.

"You are a woman after my own heart," Hamel laughed as he looked up at their waiter, "I'll have the same."

"Yes sir, 'at-sa two white-a clam sauce comin-a right up."

It had been several weeks since he met Jane Shuman. His job as a crime reporter gave him many opportunities to meet FBI Agents but none as pretty as Jane, nor as much fun to be with and the fact that she actually seemed to enjoy early diners made it much easier to be with her. After dark was usually when his job got busiest. He waited until the waiter was out of ear shot before raising his glass towards his dinner date, "Okay, Jane, to what do I owe the honor of being allowed to buy you the best Italian dinner in town?"

"Oh not so fast, Al." She lifted her glass towards him then took a sip. "If I tell you before the Tiramisu you'll probably run out of here and leave me stuck with the check."

"Would I do a thing like that?"

"Alvin, the first lesson we got at the academy was never trust reporters."

"Oh man, that really hurts Jane."

"Poor boy," Jane's voice was almost a purr as she twirled her glass, then took another sip. After a moment she asked, "Notice anything about the way I drink?"

"The way you drink?" Hamel was obviously puzzled by her question.

Swirling the wine in her glass, she looked coyly at him, "Yes... A really sharp reporter would pick up on it immediately."

"You mean the fact that you're left handed?"

"Oh, very good." Still being coy, she added, "Did you know C. Gordon Wolfe was left handed too?"

"Nooo." What she was trying to tell him hadn't quite sunk in yet. "I didn't know that…"

"Oh look," her voice suddenly changed, "Here comes dinner."

"At's-a two spaghetti wid-a-da white clam-a sauce," their very Italian waiter announced as he delivered their food. "Specialty of-a-da house. Enjoy." He poured a bit more wine into each of their glasses before asking, "Anything else-a you need?"

Jane Shuman shook her head "no," as Hamel told the waiter, "No thanks," then waited until she carefully entwined a fork full of spaghetti and put it into her mouth before asking, "So, being left handed?...."

"Oh," with some obvious excitement she wiped drops of clam sauce from her lips, "Guess what? This morning I passed my right hand test on the range. I'm a pretty good shot with my left, but right handed, wow the gun just feels so awkward..."

He began to understand, "And Gordon Wolfe shot himself on the right side of the head... with his right hand?"

"Gee," she answered as she prepared to take another bite, "You know I can't give out any information like that. You probably need to talk to the cops." She pushed the fork full of food into her mouth before adding, "I heard Tony Franco was working on the case until they decided there wasn't any case to work on."

Philadelphia, PA.

IT WASN'T until the man wearing a cowboy hat, western boots and carrying a large suit case was half way across the lobby that Lucas recognized him, "God damn, Marty, you back again? Where's your horse and where'd ya get that hat?"

"Tied my horse ta-tha light pole down stairs podna," John Gunner laughed. "Aint nobody lookin' fer him, but I kind-a like ta wear my hat when I'm 'round them see-cure-it-tee cameras." Then dropping his attempt at a western drawl, Gunner reached out to shake his hand, "It's good to see you again Lucas."

"Good to see you too Marty, or whoever you are this week, you comin' back for a while?"

"Yes, if you think it will be okay. I don't want to create any problems for you."

"I don't think it will," Lucas answered. "A lot of people stay here, we aren't supposed to know who they are, but I would kind-a like to know just what we might be getting into."

"Fair enough," Gunner looked at his watch, it was just a few minutes to seven. "You still get off at seven?"

"Yes. If Benny gets here on time and he usually does."

"Okay, let me get checked in and use the head, then I'll treat you to dinner and tell you all about it."

"Sounds good to me," Lucas agreed.

Farrell's Bar and Grill was just half a block away from The Palms and owner Jimmy Farrell was an old friend of Lucas'. As they arrived Jimmy hurried out from behind the mirrored bar, that ran half way down the narrow tile floored establishment, to warmly welcome Lucas, escort them to a corner table, and insist on serving them martinis on the house.

"I'm not much of a drinker," Gunner whispered as he took a first sip, then, "Wow! Half of this will put me under the table."

"Don't worry," Lucas gave him a wink and a nod. "We don't want to make Jimmie think we aren't grateful so fake it for a while, then we can switch glasses and I'll finish it for you."

"Then you'll be under the table," Gunner laughed.

"No, no, not me. I live on these things," Lucas assured him. "So, tell me about the FBI and why they're after you."

Gunner took another small sip of his martini, then, "Lucas, I thought about it but I can't. I could make up a story, a lot of bull shit, but you've been too good a friend for me to do that. Let me just tell you they want to talk to me about some things I simply can't tell them about." He took a third sip, "I know that isn't what you want to hear and if it is going to make a problem for you I'll get out tonight."

Lucas looked over towards the bar until he caught Jimmie Farrell's eye and signaled for a second drink before responding. "They don't know we have any connection Marty. Unless they pick you up on the security camera there's no reason for them to even look for you here… Is there?"

"No, I don't think so."

Lucas looked up as Jimmy Farrell delivered his drink, told him thanks, then turned back to Gunner. "Okay, that's good enough for me. Stay as long as you like."

Drinks and dinner finished, Gunner and Lucas thanked their host and headed out into the street without ever realizing the security camera Gunner had so easily avoided as they entered was focused on their reflection in the mirror behind Farrell's bar as they left.

Three thousand miles away a light blinked on Arnold Petrakos' PetraPad. John Gunner had been located.

Washington, DC

"DAMN IT!" Vice President Theodore Allan Dexter glared at the headline: *SUICIDE or MURDER?* then slammed his copy of the Washington Post down on his desk. He did not need this, did not need any publicity, any questions about Gordon's death. Quiet grieving, sadness, and respect are what is needed; not front page headlines and questions. When he first learned of Gordon's death he was not as surprised or shocked as he had pretended to be. He had made it very clear to Gordon that he had fucked up and needed to do something to rectify the problem. Suicide was a bit extreme, but Gordon was an impulsive man… But what if it wasn't suicide. He looked at the paper again, no question, Gordon was left handed, could he shoot himself with his right hand? Would he shoot himself with his right hand? Why? Could it be some sort of crazy attempt to stir up an investigation…? "Damn!" He said again. And what if it wasn't suicide? What if it was murder? If it was murder it had to be John Gunner. The telephone calls Gordon received from Gunner indicated he had a pretty good idea Gordon was responsible for the order on Gustafson. If Gunner eliminated Gordon would Gordon have told him anything before he was killed? That was frightening. Then, like a light bulb coming on in a dark room, he suddenly realized there might be some benefits to this situation. If they decide Gordon Wolfe was murdered, John Gunner has to be the number one suspect, an unbalanced man who had been bothering Gordon. Gordon had told them Gunner was psychotic. A prodding call to the District Police and another one to FBI Director Merrill were very much in order. They need to find this madman quickly! And when they do… a smile broke out on his face, he could imagine the scenario: disturbed man arrested for murder, a man like that is obviously a potential suicide. Yes, that would work. Unless he talked before we are able to get to him. We really need to get there first.

Philadelphia, PA

For the second day in a row much of the front page of the Philadelphia Inquirer was devoted to the mysterious death of C. Gordon Wolfe. Lucas was so absorbed in the story he was not aware of the approaching black man until he was half way across the lobby. This man did not look like a Palms guest. This man was much too… too everything. Too well dressed, too important looking, too obviously well off. So what could a man like this be doing here? Something in the back of his mind told him he knew the answer to that questions before he asked it.. Okay, let's play it cool, he told himself as he stood and took the two steps necessary to bring him up to the check-in desk

"You don't look like you're wanting a room, so what can I do for you?"

The man's face broke into a broad smile. "Jesus, that's the damnedest welcome I've ever had."

"I don't get paid to welcome people," Lucas told him. "I get paid to register people and take their money. You wanna room, forty-nine bucks, sixty-nine with a private bath."

The man's smile turned into a genuine laugh. "Okay Mr. Lucas. I'm not here to bother you, not here for a room either, just trying to locate an old friend of mine who stays here once in a while." Flipping open his PetraPad he brought up a photograph of John Gunner. "I believe you know this guy," it was a statement, not a question, "I would appreciate it if you tell him a friend of Colonel Harry's is in town and ask him to give me call." The man picked up a registration pen and held it out to Lucas. “Let me give you a number he can reach me at please.”

Very deliberately Lucas took the pen the man was holding out, then reached under the counter for a pad of yellow lined paper. “All right, what is it?”

“Six hundred; five, five, five; seven one three seven.”

“Okay.” Lucas read the number back then asked, “What‘s your name?”

“Bob,” the man answered. “But he won’t know me, just tell him I’m a friend of Harry Gustafson’s.”

Without waiting for anything further the man took a hundred dollar bill from his pocket, laid it on the counter, told Lucas, “Thanks,” then turned, walked across the lobby and quickly disappeared down the staircase.

Bill Clinton's Place

"SIX OH, OH, five fifty-five, seven one three seven ," Gunner whispered the numbers to himself as he punched them into the key pad. He had come to Clinton's Truck Stop to make the call because he knew there was a pay phone here and he knew he could get a ride to somewhere if he needed one. There was a pause after he completed entering the numbers; then the first ring… the second… half way through the third ring a voice asked "Is that you John."

"Who are you Bob?" Gunner asked. "Who am I talking to?"

"That's not important John, all you need to know is Colonel Gustafson was a friend. His death has revealed serious problems within the unit and there is a lot we need to talk about, but not on the telephone. Meet me for dinner this evening at the Oyster House, on Sansom Street, and we'll see what we can do about fixing things at Gee One."

Gunner hesitated a moment before answering. The idea of meeting some stranger who had his picture and knew where to find him was frightening. The only way he could have been found was through Computer Central...and he had been so careful. Maybe the cowboy hat didn't cover his face as well as he thought it did. Damn! But the man who was looking for him isn't one of the agents who were at Starbucks. He had seen both of them. They were both white. So "Bob" has to be someone else. Does that mean he isn't G1? Hell no. He had no idea how many agents are on the G1 roster - six, ten, fifty? Meeting "Bob" would be a crazy thing to do. But maybe… just maybe Bob is legit. Maybe he was Harry's friend, and maybe he is the contact Harry always said would show up if ever he was out of it. Maybe it’s worth taking a chance. He took a deep breath, then said, “Okay, seven o’clock.”

The Oyster House

ON A HOT muggy evening, such as Philadelphia was experiencing, the Oyster House's air conditioning did an excellent job of keeping diners pleasantly cool while the magic of dark woods and comfortable decor generally made them feel relaxed and congenial. No such adjectives described John Gunner's mental condition as he pulled the cowboy hat he was wearing down even further over his forehead and entered the restaurant. Was the brim too small to protect him? The only time he could think of when Computer Central could have found him was the other night when he checked into The Palms wearing the hat; he had been using the fire stairs since then. There was no other way they could have found him, not that he could think of anyway. And just who has found me, he wondered. The mystery voice wasn't the FBI, at least he didn't think it was, the FBI has no knowledge of G1, has it? But if it isn't the FBI, who the hell is it? Other agencies have access to the system, G1 probably has, and if that's the case what the hell am I doing here? Walking into a trap! But this might be the contact the colonel told me to expect if anything were ever to happen to him. A big "maybe," but he had to know.

A head waiter type approached, glanced at his hat and the camera hanging around his neck then said, "Welcome to Philadelphia pod-ner, "Table for one?"

"Ahhh, no. There's gonna be two of us, but he won't be here until seven or so." Gunner glanced at his watch, it was not yet six o'clock, an hour before he was supposed to meet the man. "Maybe I can find a seat at the bar to wait for him."

"Sure, no problem. Gimme your name and I'll save a table for you, seven o'clock, right?"

"Yeah, that'll be swell. Name's Brandice, Dusty Brandice."

"Got-cha." The waiter tried to hide his smile as he made a note on the slip of paper tucked into one of the menus he was holding. "See ya at seven Dusty."

The light level in the bar was low to begin with and the stool he found in the near corner was practically in the dark. It made him almost invisible while offering a direct line of site to the entrance door where would be diners waited for his headwaiter friend to welcome and seat them. He had an hour to kill, an hour to decided what he was going to do. The camera hanging around his neck was loaded and ready; would tonight be the time to use it? The time to reduce the number of agents looking for him by one? And why did he believe there would be only one man coming for him? There could be two, maybe more than that. The thought made a slight shiver run up his spine.

"What'll ya have Tex?"

The bartender's appearance caught him be surprise. "Ohh... Umm, how-bout a tall bourbon-'n-branch."

"Bourbon and water comin' up."

The thought of more than one man made him glance quickly around at the other bar patrons. There were two couples sitting near the middle of the bar and a single man at the far end. Could he be trouble? Gunner wondered.

"Bourbon and water, here ya go." The bartender put the drink down in front of him and pushed a basket of salted nuts in his direction. "You wanna run a tab?"

"Yeah, please," Gunner told him, as he laid a twenty dollar bill on the bar, then looked again towards the man at the far end. Does he look suspicious? Dangerous? He seems to be glancing in this direction. As the bartender turned away the man got to his feet. Out of the corner of his eye Gunner suddenly became aware of the man's intentions: a very attractive blonde making her way towards him and into his welcoming arms. Okay, that doesn't necessarily mean he isn't G1, but most likely he isn't. He took a sip of his drink and looked again at his wrist watch. Six-ten. He had a long time to wait. Wait for what? he asked himself. Am I here waiting for a man who wants to eliminate me when I could be heading for some place far away? No, I'm waiting here because I want to see him. I want to know what he looks like. I want to know the face of my enemy, if he is my enemy. And I want to know if maybe he is the contact Colonel Gustafson spoke about.

"Yeah, maybe," he said out loud.

"Another one?"

Surprised, Gunner looked up from his almost empty glass to the bartender standing before him. If he was going to sit here he should order another, but if he was going to be sharp he shouldn't drink it. "Yeah pod-ner," he forced himself not to laugh as he used thc headwaiter's phrase, "Another will go just right."

It was ten minutes to seven when they arrived. Two men; something about them caught his attention. They didn't look FBI, but they just didn't seem right; they didn't look like the rest of the crowd. The headwaiter checked his reservation list as he welcomed them with something approaching a flourish then escorted them to a booth on the far side of the dining room. Less than three minutes later a well-dressed, athletic looking black man arrived. A man who more or less fit the description Lucas had given him… The headwaiter immediately took the man to a table only a few feet away from the booth where the two men Gunner had been watching were seated. Gunner could not tell if there was any sign of recognition between them as the man selected the chair affording him a direct view of the entrance. This was not good. This was obviously a set up and he needed to find a way out of the trap he had stupidly put himself into. Carefully keeping his movements to a minimum, Gunner signaled the bartender. “Where’s the pistola?”

“The what?”

“You know, where ya go take a piss.”

This time the bartender couldn’t contain his laughter, “Right on, Tex. You ride on down to the end of the bar then take a left down the trail there.”

“Thanksss.” Gunner deliberately slurred his words slightly. “Be rrright back.”

“The trail” was a short hallway leading to a ladies room, a men’s room, and nothing else. There were no windows, no other doors. No windows in the men’s room either. “Fuck!”

Seated at a table that afforded him a clear view of the front entrance, the man ordered a Manhattan then turned his attention to several arriving diners; none of them was John Gunner. His cocktail arrived and the waiter asked if he was ready to order. “No,” he told him, “no,” he was waiting for another gentleman. Fifteen minutes later the man checked his watch, ordered another Manhattan, then switched on his PetraPad. No clicks, no messages, nothing since the afternoon call from Bill Clinton’s. “Damn,” he muttered as the waiter returned with his second cocktail.

After another fifteen minutes; the man signaled his waiter again.

“Yes sir, another Manhattan?“

“No, I think two is enough. I don’t know what’s happened to my friend but I’m hungry.”

"Yes sir. We can take care of that, this is the place to eat, what'll you have?"

"The striped bass sounds good to me." The waiter shook his head in agreement as he wrote on his order pad. "And while you're ordering that, tell me where's the men's room, I need to wash my hands."

"Yes sir, stripe bass comin' up and the restroom is down the hallway on the right hand side of the bar."

As was usually the case, bar business had picked up around seven and for a while the bartender forgot about his cowboy patron. When he did think of him again he realized it had been some time since he went to the toilet. "Tex" must have left while he was busy. He picked up the twenty dollar bill Tex had left under the warming glass of bourbon and water and turned his attention back to his other customers.

"It was nearly midnight when someone pounded on the stall door and a heavily accented voice demanded, "Some-a-body in dere?"

Gunner looked at his watch. Jesus, he had actually dozed off sitting on the goddamn toilet seat. Well, what the hell else could he have done? It had been more than five hours since he took refuge in the men's room. Fortunately there were two other stalls and not a lot of men wanting to use the facility, no one had bothered him.

"Yeah, yeah, be right out," he told the voice. Jesus, when he stood up his legs felt cramped and his ass was sore. Never mind that, he thought, is there anybody left in the restaurant? Specifically, are the three men from G1 still there?

No, they were not. But who were they? He had an idea how he might find out.

FBI Headquarters - Washington, DC

"A MISTER LUCAS on line four Agent Shuman." the voice on her intercom told her.

"Mister Lucas?" Jane's surprise was obvious in her voice. "Okay, put him through… "Good morning Mister. Lucas. This is Special Agent Shuman…." She listened for a moment, then, "Mister. Lucas, I'd like to get my boss on the line with us and have you tell him what you just told me. Will that be okay?"

"Yeah sure. I don't see why not," Lucas answered.

A moment later Chris picked up. "Mister Lucas, this is Special Agent Christopher please tell him what you just told me."

"Okay. Hi Agent Christopher, I was just telling Miss Shuman about this guy who came in yesterday morning. A big well-dressed black guy, said he was looking for an old friend and showed me a picture of the same man she was looking for a few days ago. I don't know if that's anything you people wan-a know, but she said I should call you if anything turned up… I probably should-a called you sooner…"

"Don't worry about that," Jane told him. "You've called and that's what counts."

"Mr. Lucas," Chris spoke up, "Do you know who the man was?"

"No, not really. He said his name was Bob and he was a friend of Gus somebody.

“Did he think you knew the man in the picture?”

“Yeah, I guess. He said he heard the guy stays here. I don’t know where he got that idea from. Maybe he did, but I can‘t remember everybody.”

“Mr. Lucas,” Jane broke in. “Do I understand this man came to the desk there in the hotel?”

“Yeah, that’s right. About ten-thirty yesterday morning.”

“Mr. Lucas, I’m going to have our computer people pull up your security camera recording. If the man is on there we may be able to identify him, if we can we may want to check his picture with you to make sure we have the right person.”

“You shouldn’t have any trouble spotting him,” Lucas said. “A black guy, wearing a business suit and a tie. Last time I saw anybody in a suit and tie was at my sister’s wedding four years ago.”

“Good enough, Mr. Lucas,” Jane laughed. “You have been a very good citizen to call us. Thank you, we really appreciate it.”

“Yes indeed,” Chris added. “We will be in touch if we have any questions and please, let us know if you have any further contacts with this man, or anyone else looking for John Gunner.”

“John Gunner, that’s his name?”

“Yes, that’s right,” Jane said. “Please let us know if you have any further inquiries.”

“I’ll sure do that Miss Shuman.”

Even before Jane hung up Chris called Norman Zight and asked him to check The Palms’ security camera recordings. Less than ten minutes later Norman returned the call.

“Believe it or not,” the pride in Norman’s voice was obvious, “We have identified the man at the hotel in Philadelphia as Ronald Chatsworth, a pilot who flies for Arnold Petrakos.”

“Surprise” barely covered Jane’s and Chris’ reaction. “Why in God’s name would a pilot who works for Arnold Petrakos be in Philadelphia looking for John Gunner?” Chris wanted to know. “How certain are you of the ID, Norm?”

“We have a pretty good picture of him from the hotel surveillance camera Chris.”

“Ummm. You know when video pictures are questioned they have a way of becoming not quite so defining.”

“Yes,” Zight’s voice sounded a little less confident as he admitted, “I do know that. Security cameras are not always positioned to make perfect close ups and I don’t expect the camera at The Palms is exactly top of the line, but the picture we got was pretty clear. It’s possible the man is just someone who looks like Chatsworth, but I don‘t think so. I think our make is good.” Zight thought for a moment, “What about the room clerk? We have good file photos of Chatsworth, would he be able to positively identify him?”

“Yes, maybe. I’m not sure he pays that much attention to people.”

“Well I’ll send you the photos if you wanna check it out.”

FBI Director Merrill's Office

THE DIRECTOR was half way out the office door when his secretary held up her telephone and waved frantically at him, "The vice president is calling, sir."

"Oh dear…" Vice President Dexter was not one of his favorite people. He looked at his watch: 11:30. He wasn't due for lunch with the Attorney General until noon so he had time to take the call. "Yes, all right. I'll be right there."

As Merrill headed back to his office he could hear his secretary, "I caught him… Please tell the vice president Director Merrill is headed back into his office to take his call."

Laying his briefcase on top of his desk, Merrill sat down and reached for his phone, "This is Director Merrill…"

"Thank you Director Merrill," the voice in his ear told him. "One moment please."

Almost immediately Dexter's voice exploded in his ear. "Merrill!"

God the man has a loud voice, "Yes Mr. Vice President. Good morning sir."

"Not all that good, Merrill. What progress are you making on finding John Gunner?"

"Well actually sir we have two agents heading to Philadelphia as we speak."

"Is that supposed to answer my question?" The vice president's voice was tinged with sarcasm.

"Sir," Merrill took a quick breath to control his anger, "We have information that John Gunner may be staying at a hotel there."

"Sounds like bull-shit. What hotel?"

"A hotel named The Palms, sir. I'll have more information as soon as the agents report in."

"Hum." The vice president's exclamation fully expressed his dissatisfaction. "That's not much news Merrill. Call me when you know something. It's time you people get off your asses and wrap this up." The vice president hung up before Merrill could reply.

Philadelphia, Pa.

SOMETIMES Agent Shuman was very happy David Christopher always wanted to drive, but not when she was anxious to get somewhere quickly. If she had been at the wheel this afternoon she would have broken every speed law in the state of Pennsylvania, but calm, steady Chris kept the needle at no more than five miles an hour above the 55 MPH limit. She couldn't help thinking that someday maybe they would really get a handle on the energy crisis and someday maybe people would be able to do 70 and 80 again, the way her mother and father once did. And just how she could be thinking thoughts like this when they might be on the verge of finding some answers to the John Gunner mystery was a question she couldn't answer. Ronald Chatsworth; Arnold Petrakos; PeTraCo, the world's leader in electronics, and heart attacks? Is that possible? She asked herself.

"What a dump," Chris's voice brought her attention back to the moment. Somehow, even with Chris' slow speed, it was only 2:30, there, just up the block, was the sign: "The P LMS," with the "A." still missing.

"Agent Shuman," the man behind the counter recognized Jane immediately, "You got here pretty quick. Any luck finding the guy?"

"Maybe," Jane smiled. "That's what we came to find out Mister Lucas. And this is Special Agent Christopher. You talked with him this morning."

"Good morning," Chris extended his arm for a hand shake

“Yeah, hi.” Lucas shook the offered hand. “Nice to meet you.”

“Mr. Lucas your security camera tape seems to identify this person…” Jane opened her brief case and produced two photographs of Ronald Chatsworth, “…as the man who was asking about John Gunner, however the video isn’t all that clear so we wanted to show you these photographs to see if you can make a positive ID on the man.”

Lucas took the two photos and looked at them carefully: one was of Chatsworth in a pilot’s uniform, the other was of him in a sport shirt. “Yeah… I think that’s the guy. He was wearin’ a business suit, but I think that’s him. What is he, a pilot or something?”

“He may be,” Chris answered. “We couldn’t confirm his ID until you could check these photos.”

Before Lucas could ask another question Jane chimed in, “I can’t tell you how much we appreciate your help Mister Lucas.”

“Yes indeed we do,” Chris agreed. “Thank you. You’ve been very helpful. If you hear any more from this man, or from Mister Gunner, please let us know, and please ask them to contact us.”

Lucas watched the two agents walk back across the lobby floor to the stairwell and disappear. Seconds later, as the buzzer announced the opening and closing of the street door he looked back over his shoulder, “So, how’d I do?”

“You should get an Academy Award,” John Gunner called from the back room.

Interstate Route 95

On the way back to Washington David Christopher again drove at a steady 55. He and Jane Shuman had discussed their amazement at the now seemingly positive ID of Ronald Chatsworth as the man who was looking for John Gunner and now both had become silent, deep in thoughts of their own. They were nearing the city when Jane's phone began to ring.

"Special Agent Shuman," she answered.

Agent Christopher could not hear the other side of the conversation and, paying careful attention to the highway traffic, he did not see the expression of amazement that slowly lit up Jane Shuman's face.

"Mr. Boyle I appreciate this very much.," Jane told the caller a moment longer. "May I ask you to please send a copy of that report to my office." Another brief pausc, then, "Thank you sir. Thank you very much." Jane closed her phone then twisted slightly in the seat to look directly at David Christopher. "That was Mr. Boyle…"

Chris waited the perfunctory five seconds for Jane to continue, then, "All right Jane, I put another quarter in the slot, now who the hell is Mr. Boyle and what does he want?"

"Oh, I thought I told you, Mr. Boyle is from Panavision, you know, the people who make cameras. Just on a hunch I asked him to check the serial number from the camera we recovered."

"John Gunner's camera?" Chris asked.

“Yes,” Jane answered, “Only no. You remember they told us Gunner brought his camera with him when he joined TVNews four years ago?”

“Yesss?…” Chris’ curiosity was obviously in full gear.

“Well Mr. Boyle says the camera we found is less than two years old.”

Director Merrill's Office

REPORTING to the director was becoming old hat. Jane sat comfortably in her chair waiting patiently for the director to finish reading something. This second visit to his office was far less stressful than the one a few days ago'

"All right Jane," he looked up at last. "What have you learned?

"Sir, Arnold Petrakos' private jet arrived at Newark Airport at 5:36 pm day before yesterday. Ronald Chatsworth was the pilot, Mrs. Petrakos and Mr. Petrakos' assistant Norma Washington were the only passengers. The two women went into New York City for some shopping, which is apparently something they do rather frequently. Mr. Chatsworth, the co-pilot, and the Flight Attendant all checked into the Red Lion Hotel there at the airport. Yesterday morning a man we have now identified as Mr. Chatsworth appeared at The Palms hotel in Philadelphia looking for John Gunner." Jane looked up from her notes, "Mrs. Petrakos and Miss Washington stayed two nights at the Waldorf Astoria then returned to the airport early this afternoon. The jet took off for a return to California as soon as they were on board."

"Well obviously the man had ample time to travel to Philadelphia if he wanted to Jane," Director Merrill's voice indicated a certain level of disbelief, "How certain are we of that identification?"

"Sir, Computer Central first ID'd him, then Agent Christopher and I traveled to Philadelphia earlier today to have the desk clerk at The Palms corroborate."

"My God." Merrill thought for a moment before asking, "Sounds pretty positive, but why? Why in the world would Arnold Petrakos' pilot be looking for John Gunner?

"We don't have an answer for that sir, but with your approval we can have San Jose talk with him."

"Yes, by all means. The sooner the better. Let me know immediately what they learn."

"Yes sir," Jane hesitated before adding, "There is one thing more…"

The director's right eyebrow elevated slightly. "Oh dear, that sounds like the intro to another bomb shell Jane… What?"

"Sir, we've learned the camera we found is not actually the camera John Gunner used."

"Oh my…"

San Jose, California

RON CHATSWORTH climbed out of the pool to find two men in business suits waiting for him. “Mister Chatsworth, I’m FBI Special Agent Morgan and this is my partner Special Agent D’Santos…” As Agent Morgan spoke both men held out their badges, “May we have a few minutes of your time sir?”

“FBI. Wow…” Chatsworth’s surprise was obvious. “Ah, yeah, sure. Let me get my towel…”

As he walked to his deck chair and grabbed a towel to dry his face with Ron Chatsworth’s mind was turning at full speed. An FBI visit was not something he had really anticipated, none the less the possibility had been considered and answers to possible questions formulated. “Okay.” He put the towel over his shoulders. “Can we talk here or would you like to grab a table and have a cup of coffee.” As he spoke he gestured towards the serving area at the opposite side of the pool.

“Right here is fine, Mister Chatsworth, we just have a couple of questions,” Agent D’Santos answered.

“We’re anxious to locate a man named John Gunner,” Agent Morgan added before Chatsworth could respond. “We understand you were looking for him in Philadelphia, day before yesterday, and we’re wondering if you had any success in contacting him?”

“John? No. I didn’t really expect to find him in Philly, he lives in Washington, but just for the hell of it I thought I’d check.”

“Did you travel to Philadelphia looking for him?” D’Santos asked.

”No…” Chatsworth laughed. “We were at Newark, Mrs. Petrakos wanted to do some shopping in New York so I had a day off. I love east coast seafood, so I took a bus down to Philly - some of my favorite restaurants in the world are in Philadelphia - anyway, when I got off the bus I didn’t see any cabs and it was a beautiful day so I decided to walk a few blocks and ran into The Palms Hotel. John had told me he stayed there once in a while - God knows why, it’s a dump - but just for the hell of it I thought I’d just check and see if he happened to be in town. He wasn’t.”

“Is Mister Gunner a close friend?” Agent Morgan asked.

“No. Not really. I met him a few months ago while we were in Washington. We had a couple of beers together and told each other we would get together again next time I was in town.”

“Is there some reason why you carry his picture with you?” Agent Morgan asked.

“Well I don’t exactly carry his picture with me,” Chatsworth laughed. “He’s in my PetraPad along with three or four hundred other people I have pictures of.”

Washington, D.C.

"TALK ABOUT your tangled webs," Jane whispered to herself as she read the report from San Jose. Arnold Petrakos' personal pilot, decorated former air force captain Ronald Chatsworth, looking for John Gunner - Wow! Just the very name "Arnold Petrakos" seemed to her to bring a whole new dimension to all this. Petrakos - the man who created the technological giant PeTraCo the company that produces countless exotic weapons systems for the army, the navy, the air force, the space program… Good God, it is mind boggling. Her thoughts were so jumbled she didn't hear her phone until it rang several times. "Oh shit, what is it?" she told the phone operator. Then, quickly, "I'm sorry, I didn't mean to be rude, I'm just busy and tired. Or is it tired and busy? Anyway, hello, this is Agent Shuman."

"There is a Mister John Gunner on the line for you. He won't give me any information but he says you will know who he is; shall I…"

"Oh my God," Jane didn't let the operator finish his sentence. "Quick! Run a trace, check satellite avail, then put him on."

"Connecting…" the operator told her.

"Mr. Gunner?…"

"Have you found out who gave the message to Lucas?" The voice in her ear asked without preamble.

"Mr. Gunner, that isn't a question I can answer right now. First I have to know where you are and when we can get together."

"And that isn't a question I can answer right now," Gunner replied. "Not until I know who was the man in Philadelphia. Can you tell me?"

"That's not information I can release at this time."

"Listen., Agent Shuman, there are people trying to kill me and somehow they found me in Philadelphia. I need to know who is he."

"Mr. Gunner, are you responsible for Gordon Wolfe's death?"

Her question, from out of nowhere as it was, caught him by complete surprise. In truth he knew he might be. Hoped he was. But that was not something he wished to share with the FBI. "Gordon Wolfe?" He exclaimed with what he hoped sounded like complete surprise. "Jesus no. Where did you get that idea?"

The click in her ear told her their conversation was over. Almost immediately her phone rang again. "Yes?"

"Call was coming from Camden, New Jersey. We'll have the exact location in a few seconds."

"Okay, thanks." She quickly punched in David Christopher's number. "Just had a call from John Gunner," she told him when he answered. "He's in Camden. Wants to know who was the man looking for him at The Palms."

Camden, N.J.

JOHN GUNNER looked unbelievingly at the phone in his hand. They were now looking at him as a suspect in Gordon Wolfe's death. That must mean they have decided his death was not suicide… He was eliminated. Hunter! The man from Starbucks, he checked into the Woodland the night Wolfe died. "Wow!" He said out loud. The distant sound of sirens intruded on his thoughts. "Oh Jesus," he muttered. They had plenty of time to trace his call, they were on the way to find him.

Leaving his half-finished latté on the table, Gunner flipped down the helmet's face mask, climbed back onto his cycle, started the engine and released the break. Lucas' cycle, he reminded himself as he turned into the street.. Thanks to Lucas he now had the perfect disguise. "Jesus, I don't know why I never thought of this before," Lucas had said before asking, "You ever ride a motor cycle?" When he answered "yes," Lucas told him to "hang on and dashed out of the room. Two or three minutes later he reappeared with a pair of black leather pants, a black leather jacket and a motor cycle helmet. A helmet with a face piece that completely covered the face. "There's a cycle down stairs in the room next to the fire door." Lucas told him as he handed him the keys. "You put the gas in it and you can use it, but be damn careful with it."

A few blocks, and much thinking later, Gunner swung into a Mini Mall parking lot. Maybe it was time to get some help. Maybe the man who said he knew Harry was the man who could help. Maybe it was time to find out. The damn cycle pants, they were really a Harley-Davidson version of cowboy chaps and they made it almost impossible for him to get to the wallet in his jeans underneath. At last he succeeded. Tucked carefully into his bill fold was the slip of paper with the phone number: 600-555 7137. He punched in the digits and waited. The number began to ring. The fourth ring was interrupted by a voice he recognized, "Who's calling?"

"I know who I am," Gunner answered. "The question is who are you Bob?"

After a short pause the voice told him, "Camden. I don't know anyone in Camden, but Philadelphia isn't far away. Is this my dinner date who didn't show up?"

"I repeat," Gunner said slowly, "I know who I am. Who are you?"

"Who I am isn't really important just now John, let's just say I'm someone concerned for your safety and has the answer to your problems. And hopefully you may be the answer to some of ours…"

Still speaking slowly, deliberately, Gunner asked, "Who were the two men with you?"

The voice seemed surprised by this question. "Two men? What two men?"

"The two men sitting in the booth just behind you; the two men who came in a minute or two before you did."

"John, listen to me, I don't know who they were, I came alone. Obviously you were there too, but I wasn't smart enough to find you."

"The FBI knows who you are," Gunner broke in. "They ran a trace on The Palms security camera tapes."

"Yes, I know," the voice said after a pause. "What sent them to The Palms?"

"What the hell do you think? I did. Now they have your picture and they have identified you. Since they know who you are, and you keep insisting you only want to help me, why can't I know too?"

"Because right now all you need to know is I am not an agent assigned to eliminate you, but we are in a position to permanently remove you from all this jeopardy."

"Now it's not just you, it's 'we.' Just who the hell are "we," and how are you going to do that?" Gunner wanted to know.

"For openers, we have removed you from Security Central's check list."

"You have, eh?"

"You don't believe me, go test it. Give a security camera a good look at you then find a safe place to watch. When you decide no one is coming for you, you will. John, we can give you a brand new identity, a new job, and together one day we will get Group One back on track."

"I already have a new identity," Gunner's voice took on an edge. "In fact I've had so many new identities lately I'm not sure who I am anymore," he looked at his wrist watch, "And I've been on this call too long. I'll contact you again tomorrow and you can tell me more about getting the unit back on track." Without waiting for any further response Gunner clicked off, slung his ever present camera back over his shoulder, pulled the face mask back down and wheeled back into the street. As he did, with flashing lights and screaming sirens, two Camden Police Cars roared by headed in the direction of the Starbucks from where he made his call to Jane Shuman.

Verrazano Bridge, New York City

STEPHEN HUNTER was beginning to feel like a yo-yo: up and down, up and down. Christ! He just got back and here he was off again. Assignments this close together did not seem like a good idea. It would have been better to bring in Paul Savage but, he remembered, Paul was somewhere in Europe. No doubt his report on seeing John Gunner was responsible for this although he failed to understand how seeing Gunner in DC led them to locating him in Philadelphia. Not important, he told himself. They locate, I eliminate, he reminded himself. He had an assignment and that was that. At least this time he could take his own car. He always liked to travel by car and this morning‘s order allowed him ample time to do so. God knows he didn't need another plane ride this week. He had spent so much of his life on planes and trains that the pleasure of being by himself, in his own automobile, choosing his own route, going at the speed he wanted, was truly a delight. Today he had selected Grand Central Parkway, then the Nassau Express Way to reach the Verrazano Bridge that stretched from Brooklyn, across The Narrows, to Staten Island. Happily it was early enough in the afternoon to avoid what would soon be horrendous rush hour traffic. In fact traffic on the bridge was so light he was actually able to take his eyes off the road, for a few seconds at a time and enjoy the fabulous view of ships in New York Harbor, the Statue of Liberty and , in the distance off to his right, the Manhattan sky line.

In no time he reached the Staten Island Expressway that would take him across the island to Goethals Bridge and the New Jersey Turnpike beyond. If he believed in such things as omens, today's omens were very good. Best omen of all, he thought, was the unusual speed with which Pete's Camera had been able to produce a wallet size photo of John Gunner from the 8X10 that had been sent to him. He took it out of his pocket, only one thing wrong with it he realized, it looks too new. It is supposed to have been in my wallet for a year or two. Okay, age it, he told himself. Easy enough; he twisted over onto one cheek and put the photo on the seat beneath him. A little creasing will work wonders. Just to speed up the process he wiggled around a bit. After a minute or two he pulled the picture out from under him, yes, very good, now it now looked a bit old and tired.

Philadelphia

JUST BEFORE crossing the Benjamin Franklin Bridge, from New Jersey into Pennsylvania, U.S. 676 gets the additional designation: “Route 30”. Kind of like me, Gunner thought, different names for the same damn road. So who am I today? He asked himself. It was a question he was not sure how to answer, and right now was not a good time to ponder it. It was nearing “rush hour” and bridge traffic was getting heavy.

Riding a motorcycle was fun but not something he had done for several years, therefore, in heavy traffic, with the late afternoon sun shining in his eyes and long shadows making visibility difficult, it was not something he was exactly comfortable with. As long as he paid close attention to what he was doing, and what the traffic around him was doing everything was okay, but when he let his mind drift off to something else, that was when trouble could begin. Trouble like the car that suddenly came out of nowhere to cut across in front of him and roar down an exit ramp. He had to break hard and swerve so sharply he could feel the bike losing it. “You ass-hole,” Gunner managed to shout after the disappearing sports car while he struggled to stay upright. No more thinking about phone calls, he told himself, right now he needed to concentrate on driving and watching for the exit to Arch Street that would take him back to The Palms.

Filbert Street

IT WAS JUST a couple of minutes past 5:30 when Stephen Hunter, now wearing his Richard Smith glasses, arrived in Philadelphia. He easily found his way to Filbert Street, turned into the parking garage and took a ticket from the automatic gate machine. The five story parking structure was only four blocks away from The Palms. The telephone voice had told him the hotel was something far less than first class so he was dressed accordingly: old jeans and a nondescript jacket he sometimes wore when he went for a hike in the country. Appropriately dressed and carrying a small satchel that had seen better days, he felt confident he looked like a person who would be seeking a room in a cheap hotel. Five minutes later he stood looking up at the hotel's battered old sign.

Gunner was surprised at how wobbly his legs felt as he climbed off the cycle. Not surprising, he realized, he had spent a lot of time on the bike and his legs were not used to it. The Palms' Emergency Exit door opened easily and he wheeled Lucas' cycle into the store room underneath the Emergency Stairs.

The Palms

WHAT DO YOU SUPPOSE he's all about, Lucas asked himself as the man came across the lobby. He was dressed like most of the hotel's guests, but the jeans, old though they might be, looked Neiman-Marcus not WallMart, and the haircut definitely was not SuperCuts.

"What can I do for you?" Lucas asked.

"Got a room for tonight? Maybe a couple-a nights. I'm trying to find an old friend a mine. He told me he stays here once in a while." The man pulled out his wallet and produced the photo of Gunner. "You don't happen to know him do you?"

Jesus, manicured nails! Definitely not The Palms type Lucas said to himself as he looked at the photo, "Umm, can't say as I do. Pretty ordinary looking guy, could be anybody I guess. I don't really pay a lot of attention to people. Single's forty-nine bucks, sixty-nine with a private bath."

"I'll take it with a bath." The man took a Visa card out of his wallet.

"Sorry, we don't use those things here, cash only," Lucas told him. "Room's available as long as you want it."

"Real money huh? Okay, works for me," Hunter said.

"Name and address and sixty-nine bucks is all I need," Lucas told him as he held a registration sheet out to the man. "Check out time is eleven AM."

As Gunner climbed the fire stairs his mind was full of thoughts about how much Lucas had done for him. The cycle, the outfit, the key to this entrance, most of all his friendship. He needed to tell him… Like most Emergency Doors, the door to the second floor lobby had a small glass window. As Gunner reached for the door handle he saw a customer standing at the registration desk talking to Lucas. He did not want to interrupt. The customer took a key from Lucas then turned towards the stairs.

Jesus Christ! It was Hunter, the man from Starbucks!

Agent Shuman's Office

JANE LOOKED at her watch, it was after six. There really isn't any "quitting time" for agents but today had been a long one and she was ready to go home. She pushed things into her brief case and was almost out the door when the phone rang.

"Damn!" Should she answer it? What difference would it make, they would catch her on her way out or call her on her cell. She walked back to her desk and answered on the fourth ring. "Shuman."

"You have a call from a Mr. Lucas in Philadelphia."

"Oh my God…. Put him on…." There was a click. "Mr. Lucas, this is Agent Shuman…"

"Hi. Listen, I hate to bother you, but you said…"

"It's never a bother to hear from you Mr. Lucas. What's up?"

"Yeah, well, a guy just checked in a few minutes ago. He showed me a picture of that man you're looking for. Asked if I knew him, said he was his friend and wants to find him…"

"You say this man just checked into the hotel?"

"Yeah, maybe ten minutes ago. Name-a Richard Smith. He's in Room 507."

All thoughts of going home were forgotten as Jane thanked Mr. Lucas then quickly clicked Norman Zight's extension. "Norman, somebody checked into The Palms a few minutes ago. Can you run a check on everybody who got there in the last half hour - see if anyone familiar turns up." Without waiting for a response Jane added she was heading for Chris' office and then probably to Philly. Please to let her know if he found anything.

Agent Christopher's Office

"NORMAN, looking for you," Chris said as he handed her the phone.

"What-cha got Norm?" Jane asked.

"Hold your hat, Jane...."

She took a deep breath... and waited. Then, "Norm. For God sake..."

"Just giving you a bit of the old Jane Shuman pregnant pause," he laughed. "So okay, we got a make on your guy and you will never believe what we turned up. The man at The Palms is Stephen Hunter, a fine arts dealer from New York..." Another pause

"Norm," an irritated Jane Shuman said. "I can tell there is more so for Christ sake tell me..."

"Yeah, Jane, there is more. The Palms' camera got several different angles of this guy and guess what - I'm certain he is the same man who was bent over Harry Gustafson's body holding a camera."

The air rushing out of Jane Shuman's lungs almost covered her words, "Oh Jesus."

Philadelphia

RICHARD SMITH sipped his martini slowly. It was not particularly good, but it wasn't bad. Nor was the restaurant. Tile floors, a big mirrored bar, far from elegant but the menu looked promising and the food he had seen delivered to nearby tables looked quite good. Good or not, it was far better than his room at The Palms. He did not like his room, not in the least. It was clean but much too small, the bathroom had only a shower, no tub, the TV was laughably tiny; staying there was not going to be pleasant. Hopefully his assignment could be completed quickly. Meanwhile there was no reason for him to stay cooped up there. He did not have clothing suitable for an upscale restaurant but he had been confident he could find something in the neighborhood - something decent - somewhere he could have a drink and a meal. The desk clerk had suggested Farrell's. It seemed a good choice. His dinner arrived - Lamb Chops, mashed potatoes, broccoli. Simple but surprisingly good. As he ate his mind wandered over what to do next. The desk clerk did not seem to know John Gunner. That did not necessarily mean John Gunner was not in the hotel but he probably wasn't. The question is will he show up here? If so, when? How long would "the voice" want him to stay here? Didn't seem as though things were going too well with the unit right now.... Senator Anderson, Harry Gustafson, Gordon Wolfe... It wasn't really his business to question these things, but still....

It was after nine o'clock by the time Richard Smith climbed back up the stairs to The Palms lobby. He wasn't much of a baseball fan but watching the Phillies game on the big TV over the bar while having an after dinner drink seemed as good a way to kill time as any. There was a new man on the desk. “Might as well check with him,” he told himself. He pulled his wallet out of his jeans pocket as he walked to the reception desk.

“Good evening,” he told the clerk. “I’m Richard Smith, room 507.” He took the picture of John Gunner out of his wallet and held it out for the clerk to see. “I’m looking for my friend. Do you happen to know him?”

Before the clerk could answer Smith was aware of two people suddenly standing next to him.

“Mr. Smith, I’m FBI Special Agent Christopher, my partner is Special Agent Shuman. We would like to ask you a few questions sir…”

San Jose, CA

ACCORDING TO Arnold Petrakos, the Hedley Club, just off the De Anza Hotel lobby, served the best Marguerites in the Silicon Valley and, being only two blocks from the PeTraCo Building, it was a regular meeting place for him and Edith when the luncheon meeting of her women's club brought her into town. There they would talk about the concerns both had regarding the world in which they live as they sipped their drinks before eventually crossing the lobby for dinner in the wonderful Italian restaurant, LaPastaia. This evening Edith was just getting warmed up on one of her particularly favored subjects, world over population, when her husband's phone began to vibrate.

"Oh, God," he groaned as he reached into his pocket. "Sorry honey…" Flipping the phone open he looked at the Caller ID. "This may be important," he told her before clicking the "talk" button to ask, "What's up?"

"John Gunner's on my line, you wanna talk to him?"

"Yes. Put him on, Ron." He listened to a couple of clicks then asked, "Is that you John?"

"What if I say it's Richard Smith?" the caller answered. Edith could not hear the caller's voice but she knew from her husband's reaction that he had said something Arnold did not expect.

"Where did you get that name from?" Petrakos asked after a second.

"He just checked into the same hotel I'm in. I thought his name was Hunter, but what-a I know. Does he work for you?"

"Not exactly," Petrakos answered, "Although I can cancel his mission."

"Jesus." Gunner muttered.

Petrakos waited for a further response, when none was forthcoming he said, "It's time to take me up on our offer, John. You've done your job. You opened the can of peas and showed us what's gone wrong with the unit. Now it's time to let someone else clean up the mess. I can send Richard Smith - Hunter away and make sure nobody else is on your back."

'How you gunna do that?" Gunner asked. "And just who the hell are you?"

"How isn't really important John, nor is who I am You'll probably find out some day but if you don't it won't make any difference as far as your future is concerned. Trust me, John."

For a moment he thought Gunner had hung up, then, in a very resigned voice, he heard him say, "Okay."

Washington, DC

AGENTS Shuman, Christopher, Winter and Computer Technician Zight stood respectfully awaiting the arrival of Director Merrill. The unexpected, early morning hurry up summons to the meeting had caught them all by surprise. Agent Winter looked questioningly at David Christopher but got only a shoulder shrug in response, a moment later, with a very serious look on his face, Director Merrill joined them. "Sit down," he nodded towards the chairs surrounding the conference table, "Sit down everyone." The director remained standing as they did so. "What I have to tell you this morning is very serious and very confidential; it must not leave this room." He looked slowly at each of his four listeners, then added, "There must be no slip-ups." He paused again. "I would like each of you to acknowledge your understand this.... Special Agent Christopher?"

"Yes sir, I understand..."

Special Agent Shuman?..."

"Yes sir. I understand..."

"Special Agent Winter?"

"I understand..."

"Technician Zight - you perhaps more than anyone must fully understand."

“Yes sir.” Obviously flustered by having been singled out, Norman Zight blinked, nodded his head and raised his right hand. “I understand.”

“Very good.” The director leaned forward placing his knuckles on the table top. “I have just been talking with the attorney general. He has advised me, and I am advising you, that as of this moment our pursuit of John Gunner and our investigation into his activities is ended. The matter has been placed in the hands of another agency.”

The collective, shocked gasp from all at the table was not unexpected. Director Merrill waited patiently as his listeners looked at each other, then back to him. “I will add only this,” the director continued after a moment, “This is a matter of national security. I know I can count on each of you to keep your silence.” He again scrutinized his listeners before telling them “Thank you,” then turned and left the room.

After several seconds of stunned silence, in a voice loud enough for all to hear, Special Agent Jane Shuman spoke for everyone in the room, “Oh Shit!!!”

JUNE

Apartment #3 - Cherry Avenue

TWO WEEKS LATER Beryl Kinney's search engine produced an item from the Philadelphia Weekly "Police Reports" column:

Police Seek Vehicle Owner
A 2009 Subaru Forester abandoned at the North Philadelphia Airport has been traced to Albert Helms of Staten Island, N.Y. Vehicle was purchased In Pittsburgh, PA, but address shown on registration does not exist. Anyone with information about Mr. Helms is asked to contact the Philadelphia Police Department.

July

Office of the Vice-President

LOOKING AT Theodore Allan Dexter seated behind his magnificent mahogany desk, silver hair combed so carefully, strong, square jaw set so confidently; blue eyes - bright blue eyes that assured you behind them was an IQ well over 200; looking at him seated there AllWorldOil's President Donald Harris thought the vice president of the United States looked every bit the wise leader he knew him to be. Thanks to Dexter's genius, Harris could not help mentally rubbing his hands together, thanks to Ted's genius he too had actually joined the Billionaires Club. Supposedly, as vice president of the United States, Theodore Allan Dexter no longer had any involvement in AllWorld but Don Harris knew that deep in his heart, and deep in his bank account, Ted Dexter was still a company man. A company man now in position to insure the company's profitability to a degree few thought possible. And if by some chance Ted Dexter should one day become president... The very thought made Don Harris tingle. And it might not be so unlikely. Ted had told him - in strictest confidence - the president has some heart problems. Problems she, and the entire administration, would quickly deny, but still...

"Don," the Vice President said after a moment of thought. "I'm disappointed in you; disappointed in your whole approach to this situation."

"Oh?..." Harris was surprised by Dexter's vehemence.

"Yes indeed. Now listen to me. I want you go into that committee room next week and take the high ground! I want you to tell that ass-hole Elwood Stone, and Chip Young, and the rest of those..."

Dexter pushed his lips in an out three times before selecting the word he wanted, "…those senators, that you are extremely upset by their questioning AllWorld's integrity. You tell them AllWorldOil has done, and is doing, everything possible to insure the United States of America has sufficient oil to maintain its way of life while the entire country waits for congress to do something constructive by way of making this nation energy independent. You tell them they have failed! For years and years they have completely failed to fund serious alternate energy projects, all the while continuing to refuse us drilling rights here in our own land. If that means we have to deal with some middle-eastern people they don't approve of… well they should thank God we do, and they should investigate themselves, damn quickly! Tell them they should be singing our praises, not calling you down here to justify how we… um, how you, conduct business." Dexter thought for a moment before adding, "And you just might suggest to Senator Young that he ought to have better things to do in his new job than trot out some of his old boss' fantasies about AllWorld keeping the war going…just what the hell Governor Updike was thinking about when he appointed an idiot like Young is beyond me…"

A knock at the door interrupted Dexter's tirade and a second later Mildred Thomas, the vice president's secretary stuck her head into the room. "It's almost one o'clock, Mr. Vice President. Your car's waiting..."

"Thank you, Mildred," he told her in that deep, warm, wonderfully sincere voice Donald Harris so envied, "Be right there." Then turning to his old friend, he said, "Gotta chase you out of here Don, I'm heading for a golf tournament out in sunny California. You take care of things with Chip Young and his friends. As Harry Truman used to say, 'Give 'em hell!'"

San Jose, California

JOHN GUNNER glanced at his wrist watch: 7:45. With Press Check-in scheduled for three o'clock this afternoon he knew he could have a real shave before hitting the road and still have plenty of time for "sight-seeing" once he got there. There was something about shaving with soapy lather and a razor that he always found pleasing. Sure, his electric razor did a pretty good job, and he could always use it when in a hurry, but lather and a razor blade always made him feel cleaner… better shaved. And it always gave him what his mother used to call "rumination time." A lot had happened to him in the few weeks since he made that phone call from Philadelphia, a lot to "ruminate" about. Officially he did not yet know his mysterious benefactor - his new control officer, the metallic voice on the telephone. He had an idea who it might be but if the voice didn't want to be known that was okay, so far the voice had kept every promise. "More than," Gunner said half out loud: The flight to San Jose in a private jet; another new identity - he was now John Marshal - this great apartment, a good job, and now payback time. He did not believe in an "after life," but if there was such a thing he hoped Colonel Gustafson would be watching. It seemed as if everything was perfect but somewhere in a back corner of his mind Edward Spalding could hear his mother saying, "*If it sounds too good to be true, it probably isn't true.*"

His new control officer had assured him this would be his final assignment, the end of Group One, but just what did that mean? Something about the new camera that had been delivered last night bothered him: This camera had no rear chamber for a digital card. This camera had a slightly different eye piece, and he was certain it contained a built in location chip. No doubt the new camera would produce the desired end result, but who's desire? Would it be a result he would be happy with? What would happen if two heart attacks were to occur at the same moment… Jesus, that would certainly cause some raised eyebrows. If that were to happen raised eyebrows would not do him any good, but it would certainly have been his final assignment..

Looking at himself in the mirror he twisted his mouth to permit the blade to slide more easily over the taught skin around his upper lip and found himself beginning to grin. He was certain the voice didn't know about the quick trip he had made to DC to pick up his old video camera and the power cards the night before his plane ride to California. Nobody had looked at his luggage; nobody knew he had it. Maybe the new camera was good as gold, nothing to worry about, but he did not know the new camera; he did know his own camera. And he was certain of the results he could achieve with it.

"Okay, enough of this shit," he told himself as he glanced at his wrist watch again. He had made his plans with great care. It was time to stop screwing around, time to strap on his money belt, put on a shirt, gather up his things and be on his way.

Moments later, as he headed up the On Ramp to the 280 Freeway, his phone buzzed.

"Hellooow."

"It's me John."

"My God, I was just thinking about you, Sonja." Actually he had not been thinking about her at all. Sonja Davis was the Assistant Assignment Editor at KSAN-TV. There had been a certain mutual attraction between them since they first met when he reported for work at the station but so far it had resulted in nothing more than after work drinks at "The Grill" a couple of times. Why was she was calling him? "What's up?" He asked.

“Nothing, just checking. Always wanna be certain my people are okay and covering their assignments. Where are you?”

“I’m half-way to Pebble Beach,” Gunner chuckled.

“My God, why so early? You don’t have to be there until three o’clock.”

“Yeah, but I hear it’s a beautiful place and I’m into sightseeing.”

“That’s cool,” she told him.

“Cool maybe,” he said, “But I think I would rather be in San Jose tonight having a drink with you. Couldn’t I…”

“Don’t even think about it, John,” she broke in. “In our business the news comes first. Besides, I have a headache,” she added with a laugh. “Call me when you get back.”

“Okay. See ya.” Thinking to himself, I’m gonna miss you, he clicked off.

Fenwick Island - Delmarva Peninsula

JANE SHUMAN looked out the window at the sand dunes and the ocean beyond. Delaware, Maryland, and Virginia: Del-Mar-Va. Just how in the world of politics, she wondered, did those states agree to divide up such a lovely strip of land and let it be named after all three? Obviously it happened long before today's state of argumentative disagreement between all elected representatives of the people. No matter, she loved the peninsula and had ever since her father bought the cottage on Fenwick Island. As a child it was here that she, her mother, and her brother spent their summers while her hard working father endured the heat of Washington. Fortunately DC is close enough that he had been able to spend most weekends with them. It had been his plan to retire one day then he and her mother were going to spend summers on Fenwick Island, winters in Sarasota, Florida. There had been times when Jane wished her mother would have sold the place after her father died; being here brought back so many memories. She blinked her eyes, those were days too precious to remember without tears welling up, but today she was happy her mother had kept the cottage. Memories can be beautiful, and few places can be as peaceful as the Delmarva Peninsula and Fenwick Island. The three day, 4th of July weekend was just what the doctor ordered and this was the perfect place to spend it; the perfect place for her to wind down; the perfect place to finally let go of the John Gunner investigation and come to grips with herself; with her career; with her life. Was the FBI what she wanted for the rest of her life? She would never violate the official secrets oath she had taken, but she was not sure she could any longer live with the Gunner situation. She was still young enough, and smart enough, to be successful elsewhere. She had a law degree and she had occasionally been a TV spokesperson for the bureau, maybe there was a career potential for her there. Once a TV newsman had actually told her she should give up being a G-Man and try her hand at television. And what about a husband and children? Was her mother right when she told her not very many men would be interested in a girl who carried a gun? Well, this long weekend at the cottage with her mother and her brother and his family would give her time to think more about such things.

Looking out the large picture window at her two young nephews playing in the sand, with gentle Atlantic Ocean waves breaking on the beach a hundred or so yards beyond them reminded her of the fun she and her brother used to have here… in spite of Assawoman Bay. A smile broke out on her face, how could anyone have given such a name to the lovely body of water that separates the peninsula from the mainland? When they were kids her brother made her life miserable by teasing her with that name. He would ask her questions like "What's the capital of South Dakota?" when she didn't know he would scream, "Never Assawoman anything." Her eyes refocused on the two boys outside the window, she decided it was time to join them for a swim…

Pebble Beach, California

THE HOUSE PHONE next to his computer keyboard rang softly. Arnold Petrakos typed in a few more letters before answering, "What's up Dex?"

What's up?" His house guest's voice was alarmingly chipper. "We're supposed to tee off in a couple-a hours, let's get going."

"Alright, alright, hold your horses. Some of us have to work for a living you know. I'll be with you in five minutes."

"That little 'have to work' jab will cost you two strokes a side, Arnie. Now get your ass in gear and get down here."

"Yes, right, Mr. Vice President. Be there in just a second."

Petrakos switched off the phone before the vice president could make further comment. He was almost finished; in fact… two more clicks… he was finished; the problem was about to be solved. He re-read the message he had typed: "*Assignment completion anticipated in next two hours,*" then clicked "send."

FBI Building - Washington DC

DAVID CHRISTOPHER knew why he was in the office today, Jane Shuman needed a few days off. And it wasn't too much of a sacrifice; his kids had daytime things of their own to do, and they were all going to watch fireworks at the band concert this evening. What surprised him was the fact that Director Merrill was also in the office. "Somebody has to keep an eye on things," Merrill laughingly told Chris when he called to ask him if he wanted to get together for lunch. Wilson was a good friend and the occasional lunch they managed to have together was always something David Christopher enjoyed, even today when their conversation had mostly been about John Gunner and Jane Shuman's reaction to the order to drop the case.

"Sometimes executive decisions about matters of national security are hard to understand," Merrill said as he and Chris headed back to their offices. Chris agreed this indeed was true but he wondered if he would ever be able to convince Jane to accept that fact; to let it go and move on. His mind was so occupied with thoughts about executive decisions, national security, and Jane Shuman that he was unaware Norman Zight was sitting in his outer office until Norman stood up and greeted him,

"Hello Chris."

"Norman. What are you doing here today?"

"I need to talk to you, something's come up." The man was obviously a bit anxious.

“Come on in and have a seat,” Christopher told him in an effort to make him more comfortable. “What’s up?”

Zight waited until the door was closed and they were both seated before starting to answer Chris’ question. “Something pretty strange,” he began slowly. “I’m not sure if I should bother you with this, Chris, but Jane isn’t here today…”

As Zight’s voice trailed off, Chris tried to reassure the man: “You’re never a bother, Norm.”

“I hope not. Anyway, something strange popped up on the computer a little while ago and I thought you might want to know about it…”

“Yes?..” Jesus, Chris thought to himself, get on with it.

“You know a while ago we took that John Gunner person off the watch list…”

Suddenly David Christopher was all attention. “Yeah, what about it?”

“Well, a couple of times after that Jane asked me where he was. Each time I told her he is off the list and out of the file, but believe it or not, Chris, a little while ago I think we got a click on him”

“You did?”

“Yeah… sort of. I’ve been tinkering around with that computer a lot - you know that’s what I do for fun - and a few minutes ago I had a “possible” click on him out in California, at Pebble Beach, where they’re playing that big First Tee tournament Vice President Dexter is playing in. I couldn’t get it back so I wasn’t able to confirm the hit, but I thought Jane would be interested…”

Norman Zight did not notice David Christopher's widening eyes but was fully alert to his stern voice, "Norman. You are aware the director canceled that investigation and declared any further activity would be considered a breech of National Security, are you not?"

"Yes, but…"

"There are no 'buts' on this one Norman. Now stop fucking around with the computer and forget John Gunner! And that is an order," Christopher added.

Fenwick Island

STILL STANDING at the picture window, still thinking it was time for a swim with the kids, but somehow a bit too lazy to head for the beach, Jane smiled a contented smile; it was great having the family together. Her mother loved her grandchildren and, indeed, she loved them too. Her sister-in-law, Meg, was wonderful, a good friend; and her brother, her strong, handsome big brother, she loved him dearly; none the less he could still get under her skin; he could still be a pain in the Asawoman. For example, the God damn TV golf program he was watching. There he sat on the living room sofa, ready to spend this beautiful afternoon watching the damn thing as if he expected to see the second coming. What could possibly be more boring than watching a bunch of men trying to put a little white ball in a hole? Every one of them did exactly the same thing and every golf announcer said exactly the same thing: "On this course you must keep the ball in the fairway…" Good Lord.

"Enough golf already," she told herself, and turned away from the window. It was time for that swim with the kids. As she started towards the front door the golf announcer was saying something about the number of photographers on hand waiting for the appearance of the vice president. She glanced over her brother's head at the picture on the giant TV screen and her heart stopped for a moment. "Oh my God…" she spoke out loud.

"Go! Get out! You don't have to watch," her brother shouted without turning to look back at her.

Transfixed, she stared at the screen. Would they show the lineup of cameramen again? Was it possible the man in the blue cap was him? She knew Chris was on duty today. It should have been her, but gentleman that he is, good friend that he is, he had offered her the three day holiday; a holiday she badly needed, but holiday or not an agent is never really off duty. She went quickly into her bedroom, closed the door and punched Chris' number into her palm phone.

"Chris, the golf at Pebble Beach, I think I just saw John Gunner… the man was only on the screen for a second or two, but I'm pretty sure it was him."

"Jane," She had never heard his voice sound quite so stern before. "We have been instructed to forget John Gunner and everything about that investigation. We have been advised any further involvement will be considered a breach of national security. Now please stop watching television and go enjoy your holiday."

"Shit!" Hurt and angered by Chris' reaction to her call, Jane stamped her foot and threw her phone against the wall. After a moment she returned to the living room to watch her brother's TV golf program.

Pebble Beach Golf Links

PRECEEDED AND FOLLOWED by Secret Service vehicles, the vice president's limo made its way along the driveway past dozens of happy, smiling spectators, to the edge of the practice green.

"Here we are, Arnie…"

"Right. You go ahead and get out first Dex. I'll wait a minute, I don't want people asking who that is with Arnie Petrakos."

"You son-of-a-bitch," Vice President Dexter laughed. "That's another stroke a side."

In the press section alongside the putting green John Gunner checked his camera then lifted it back to his shoulder. As the audience applauded the arrival of the vice president he put his eye in the finder and focused on the area where two steps led golfers up to the putting surface.

Fenwick Island

JANE SHUMAN WATCHED the smiling vice president waving and nodding to people as he moved through the crowd surrounding the putting green. She watched as he pulled a putter out of the bag his caddy carried, watched him drop three golf balls on the green and prepare to put.

Pebble Beach

HIS OLD CAMERA felt comfortable on his shoulder. There is nothing like an old friend, Gunner told himself. The new camera that had been delivered to him before he left for Pebble Beach was in the van he had driven. He was sure that camera had a built in location device and if anyone were checking they would know the camera is not where it is supposed to be. But there isn't a hell of a lot they can do about it now he thought as he carefully centered the crosshairs on the vice president's cheek.

"This is for the colonel, you son of a bitch!" he whispered, then squeezed the trigger.

Fenwick Island

JANE'S EYES WIDENED as she saw the vice president flinch slightly then brush his hand at what might have been a mosquito or bug of some kind on his cheek… "Oh sweet Jesus" she whispered.

"Shut up and go away!" her brother shouted.

Transfixed, Jane watched as the vice president seemed to lose his balance… What a moment ago had been applause from the crowd became a collective groan as he stumbled and fell to the ground.

Pebble Beach

IN THE CONFUSION that followed the vice president's collapse "John Marshall" was just one of the TV Cameramen jostling with each other struggling to get pictures as security people surrounded the fallen man and medics rushed to his side. Quickly, but carefully, they lifted him onto a gurney and hurried him to a waiting ambulance. Cameramen and reporters ran to their cars and vans, intent on following the ambulance. John Marshall was one of the last to follow.

Cherry Avenue

THE FAMILIAR VIBRATION under her left arm took Beryl Kinney's attention away from the television screen she had been watching intently for the past several hours. So far the news had not announced the vice president's death, something she was certain had occurred almost immediately after his collapse on the putting green. The Eschelon message she received was not in code: *Albert Helms flying this evening United Airlines Monterey - LA - Buffalo.*

Special Agent Christopher's Office

"I DON'T WANT you to do this, Jane." David Christopher looked up from the neatly prepared, carefully worded letter of resignation on his desk to the determined looking woman standing before him "You are too good an agent. You have a brilliant future with the FBI."

"Thank you, Chris. Those are kind words and I appreciate them but I simply can't do this anymore." There was no indecision in her voice. "I can't just look away and forget everything."

"Jane," Chris shook his head in exasperation, "For Christ sake sit down and let me talk some sense into you!" In response to his request she lowered herself onto a chair but did not sit back, did not relax, instead, with her spine straight, almost stiff, she sat on the front edge of the seat.

This is hopeless, Chris realized, but still he wanted to try. "Jane, I understand your thinking but believe me, the Secret Service people have been all over this thing. The vice president succumbed to a perfectly natural heart attack. I know this is hard to believe but every medical examiner confirms it. End of story."

"Maybe for you, Chris, but not for me... I think John Gunner was one of the cameramen there. I think he 'eliminated' the vice president, and I think you do too. And what about Richard Smith - Stephen Hunter? Why can't we look into that? I understand the need for national security but I also believe our laws should apply to everyone. I don't want to be part of an agency that does not subscribe to my principles."

“Okay, Jane.” Chris’ tone of voice signaled surrender. He realized there was no hope, she was determined. “What are you going to do?”

“Chip Young, I should say ’Senator Young’, has offered me a job. He wants to do some research on AllWorldOil’s activities in the middle east; sounds like it might be fun. I start in three weeks.” A tiny smile began to creep over her face, “Between now and then I’m going out to California. I’ve always wanted to see San Francisco, Big Sur and all that coast. I understand it is truly beautiful out there.”

As she was speaking Chris’ expression became more serious than she had ever seen before. “Let well enough alone Jane,” he said slowly. “Don’t go sticking your nose into things out there.”

“Is that an order, Chris?”

“No Jane, it is a warning.”

August

Toronto, Canada

THE SUN on his back was pleasingly warm and the Café Latte was just as good as the ones they served in DC. What had been surprising to John Gunner was finding a Starbucks here in Canada. It's a small world, he thought. Finding the Starbucks had been a bit unsettling at first, there were some bad memories associated with Starbucks, at least the one across the street from The Place. But that was long ago. He took a sip of his Latte, still too hot…

The trip to Canada had been far less a problem than he thought it might be. In fact his biggest problem, and the time of greatest concern, was the hour and a half he had to wait for the flight out of Monterey that took him to Los Angeles where he boarded a plane that eventually brought him to Buffalo, New York. He had used his Albert Helms, Staten Island ID. There had been no raised eyebrows, no questions asked.

In Buffalo he had taken a bus to Tonawanda where he presented the Albert Helms Pass Port and purchased a ticket for a tour of Niagara Falls; a tour that was packed with families, and newlyweds, and people of all ages; a tour that was only one of dozens of such tours, with hundreds of people anxious for a visit to Canada and a look at the falls from the Canadian side of the river; a short visit that did not often entail prolonged examinations of visitor's documentation. Once across the border it had been easy. There was no Langhorn/Davis in Canada. There were security cameras but there was still a right to privacy in Canada and Canadian cameras were not connected to Washington's Security Central; The only problem now facing him was what to do with the rest of his life. Was there a way he could become a Canadian Citizen? Was there a way he could make a living in Canada? These were question that bothered him, but not too much, not yet, the future was still a ways off. For now, he had plenty of money. He tried the Latte again, cool enough to drink now. He settled back in his chair, enjoying the sunshine…

"Hello John."

The voice startled him. A voice that seemed familiar… He took his hand away from the coffee and put it on the camera hanging at his chest. Then he turned slowly to look over his shoulder. "Beryl! My God, Beryl. What are…"

"Hi John," she interrupted. "May I join you?"

"Yeah, sure, of course." Looking quickly left and right he got to his feet as she walked towards the table.

"Not to worry," she said easily. "I'm all alone." She gave him a quick kiss on the cheek then sat in the seat opposite him. "How are you? How have you been?"

"Beryl. Don't play games. Why are you here? How did you find me?"

"How we found you isn't important, John." She reached out and put her hand on his. "Why I'm here is."

He waited for her to continue… "All right, all right. For Christ sake Beryl…"

"John, I'm with a very special agency that has need of your services. Are you interested?"

The White House

READING THE WORDS on her screen, “He is interested,” brought a smile to the president’s face. “Good job, Beryl,” she said quietly. “Very good job.”

The End